CW00864778

Female Truckers Fight Club

Joe Smith

Copyright 2022 Joe Smith

Table of Contents

Chapter 1 – The Origins

It had all started in 1977. John Drury was hauling potatoes from the Midwest to New York. Across the road from his delivery point, he saw a small adult shop and decided to check it out while his truck was unloaded. This was not like the adult shops he was used to. It focused only on the female fighting genre. He browsed for a bit before picking out a mud wrestling video tape, shot at a Los Angeles hotel, and a female fighting magazine. The sexy sales lady rang up his items before producing another video tape from a box behind her.

'This landed earlier today. It is a new topless boxing tape from Germany. Their previous tape sold out quickly. Maybe you will be interested in it.'

John took the video from her and read the description at the back. It was a topless boxing tournament with mainly German fighters. It impressed him when he saw almost four-thousand spectators bought tickets for this tournament.

'If you buy it, you may well be the first American to own this tape.'

He glanced at the price. 'What the hell. I only visit New York every so often. I think my wife will also find the female boxing interesting.'

'Is she a boxer?'

'No, but she has been in a few fistfights and she mud wrestles every time we go to a biker rally.'

'You are a lucky guy.'

'I am indeed.'

John paid for his items and returned to his truck, eager to watch the videos with his wife, Sandra. But he had a few days on the road before he would see her again. That night, he phoned her from a truck stop and told her about the videos. This built-up anticipation in both of them. Like her husband, Sandra loved watching women fight each other, almost as much as she loved fighting another woman.

When John got home, they watched the mud wrestling video first. Although it was good, they could not wait to watch the topless boxing video, as this was something neither of them had seen before. They loved it. Tits and fists were flying all over the place as beautiful women squared off to box it out. After watching the last fight on the tape, they hurried to the bedroom, where they made love for the next few hours.

Afterwards, while both were smoking a cigarette in bed, Sandra cleared her throat. 'I think I will be good at that.'

'At what?'

'Topless boxing.'

'Are you serious? Is that something you would do?'

'I tell you what. You buy me boxing gloves and a heavy bag so I can practice, and I will box any opponent you find.'

'Deal.'

'Deal.'

The very next day, John went to the shops and found a second-hand heavy bag and a pair of red boxing gloves. He had hoped to find purple gloves, but the choice was between red and black. He hurried home and hung the heavy bag in their garage before calling his wife.

'Come with me. I have a surprise for you in the garage.'

'Yippee, a new bike,' she said jokingly.

'No, even better.'

Sandra smiled broadly when they entered the garage. 'I see you are eager to see me boxing another chick topless.'

'You know I am.'

She winked at him before putting the gloves on. This took much longer than either of them expected. When they were eventually laced up, John looked at her with a frown on his face. 'Urm.'

'What?'

'You are a topless boxer. Why do you still have a top on?'

'The tits come out only when I fight another chick. But I will make this onetime exception because you spoiled me with these goodies.'

They struggled to get her top's sleeves over the boxing gloves. Sandra suggested she would practice topless for him on another day. But because he would leave the next morning for five days on the road, John persisted until he eventually got the top free from the gloves. With a smug expression on his face, he unhooked and removed her bra.

For a forty-year-old, her D-cup breasts were remarkably firm and unaffected by gravity. Her dark nipples were always eager to jump to attention, and that day was no exception.

John quietly watched while his topless wife pummelled the heavy bag. She was serious about exercise and he knew better than to disrupt her in any way. He watched her beautiful breast jiggle and bounce around as she danced around the heavy bag, hitting it with all her might. Around thirty minutes later, with her body drenched in sweat, Sandra shook her arms before asking John to help her remove the gloves.

'That was the sexiest thing I've ever seen. I need you now.'

Sandra could see the lust in his eyes. She was also horny, so she opened her arms, beckoning him in. He picked her up and pushed her up against the wall, fumbling with her skirt and panties before dropping his jeans and underpants. They made love against the wall, with the boxing gloves still on Sandra's hands. That night, they made love a few more times.

The next morning he hit the road, disappointed that he would not see his wife practice again for at least five days. He used the time on the road to work on a plan to find his lovely wife an opponent. At first, he considered placing an ad in the local paper, but he was concerned this might attract weirdos. He also did not want everybody in their small town to know about their private lives. But he could not come up with a better plan and was disappointed with himself when he pulled into the truck stop. After booking into a room, he headed to the pub to have dinner and a few drinks. As usual, a stripper was entertaining the dozen or so truckers relaxing in the pub. When he sat down at the bar counter, he heard two guys talking about the stripper.

'Didn't she use to strip at biker rallies?'

'Yes, I think her name is Ruby. My wife once had a mud wrestling match against her at a rally. She is actually a feisty little wrestler. But my wife still beat her.'

John thought about asking the stripper whether she would box his wife. But he knew this would cost him a pretty penny. Then it hit him.

'Excuse me. I could not help but to overhear you. You said your wife mud wrestled the stripper?'

'Yes, my wife enters the mud wrestling competition at every biker rally we go to.'

'Maybe she has wrestled my wife at a rally. She also enters all the mud wrestling contests.'

'You guys are so lucky. My girlfriend does not even want me to watch a strip show, let alone a mud wrestling match,' said the guy sitting between them.

'I am lucky indeed. I bought a topless boxing video the other day. After my wife saw it, she agreed to do a topless boxing match if I can find her an opponent.'

'My wife would totally do that. She loves to beat up other women while I am watching.'

'Has she done any boxing before?'

'No, but she had been in a few fistfights and many mud wrestling matches.'

'So has mine. I bought her a heavy bag and gloves yesterday. She was so excited to try boxing that she started hitting the bag as soon as I brought it home.'

'I think our wives will hit it off. Or maybe they will hate each other for being so similar. Either way, I think they will have one hell of a boxing match against each other.'

'John.' John offered his hand to the other guy.

'Dave, and this is my friend Adam.' He motioned to the guy sitting between them.

They shook hands before continuing their conversation.

'Are you serious about your wife wanting to box?'

'Yes. She started practicing yesterday and I am sure she will be punching the heavy bag every day until she has a fight. She is very competitive and once she has set her mind on something, she is all in. At the moment, her mind is on a topless boxing match. And yours, do you think she will do it?'

'I am sure, but there is only one way to find out.' Dave got up and walked to the payphone. After dialling, he waited a moment before talking. 'Hi babes, what are you doing?'

He was quiet while she talked.

'I met a guy whose wife wants to do a topless boxing match. She is looking for an opponent.'

He listened again before turning to John. 'How big is your wife?'

'About five seven and around a hundred-and-thirty-pounds.'

'Did you hear that, babes? She is about your size.'

He turned to John again. 'What is her age?'

'Forty.'

'She is two years older than you, babes.'

He listened for a while before telling his wife he loved her and that she was the best. 'She is interested, but she needs a few weeks to practice and she wants to meet your wife before agreeing to fight.'

'I am sure my wife would like to meet her first as well.'

'Do you have a venue?'

This is one thing John thought about a lot while driving. 'We could do it in my garage, or we may actually do it at a truck stop where there is a lawn. We can park the trucks to form some kind of circle or square. The women can then box each other between the trucks.'

'I like the second idea. But we will have to refine it to ensure they can fight in private and that they are safe. We don't want them to slam each other into the trucks.'

'Will you guys allow spectators? I will pay to watch them fight.'

The two husbands thought for a while. Up to now, the idea was to have the two wives fight while the two of them watched. But it would be even better if they could make money from the fight.

'Adam, do you think more guys would be interested in watching them box each other?'

'I think all the guys at any truck stop would pay to watch a fight like that.'

'What do you think, John? I think I could convince my wife to fight with a crowd watching, if we divide the ticket money between them as a reward for being willing to entertain the boys.'

'Both our wives have done plenty of mud wrestling matches. We both know how quickly they get nude during these matches. So, I don't think fighting topless with men watching would bother either of them. I agree, fighting for prize money would motivate both of them. I think seventy percent for the winner, thirty percent for the loser.'

'I agree. How do we agree who the winner would be? We can't be the judges, and I do not know whether I would trust any of the spectators to judge.'

'I have not thought about this. Maybe they fight until one is knocked out or knocked down, say three times.'

'That sounds promising. Maybe we limit it to a certain number of rounds. If they have an equal number of knockdowns, they fight a final round. If there is still no winner, we declare it a draw.'

'Yes, then they can split the money fifty-fifty.'

'If we have spectators, we can use four trucks to make a square. The spectators can then spread out to ensure they cannot smash each other into the trucks.'

'Maybe we can park a few trucks facing in on one side of the square. We can turn their lights on to ensure we all can see the action clearly.'

'I think we have a brilliant plan already. Let's exchange numbers and call signs. We can then refine this over the next week. After that we can compare our schedules and find a date when we will be in the same region. We can then make the final arrangements and inform any truckers who are interested to watch.'

'It sounds good. I think we should only invite truckers as spectators, though.'

'I agree.'

'What about truckers' wives?' The female voice behind them surprised them.

They turned around to see Ruby behind them. She was still only wearing a thong and pasties covering her nipples.

'Are you a trucker's wife?' Dave was slightly surprised.

'Yes, my husband is over there. He was a referee for amateur fights, you know.' She pointed to a guy drinking alone at a table. 'I go on the road with him and dance at the truck stops. This way I get to do what I love to do and he gets somebody to talk to and to sleep with on the road.'

'So, you are interested in watching two women box each other topless. Maybe you are interested in boxing as well?' John was hopeful.

'I want to see this first. Maybe I will try it later, but for now I only want to watch.'

'Fair enough. I think we will definitely allow biker's wives and maybe even girlfriends. Maybe you can be the topless round girl.'

'Will you pay me?'

'No, but we will allow you and your husband free entry if he is also willing to act as referee.'

'Sounds good to me. I will talk to him and let you know.'

Soon, most truckers in the pub were talking about the upcoming topless boxing match. A week later, John and Dave brought their wives with on a day when they were delivering in the same town. The two women sized each other up when they met at a truck stop pub afterwards.

'This is my wife, Eileen. Babes, this is John.'

'Hi, Eileen. This is my wife, Sandra.'

The two women shook hands, each giving the other only a brief smile.

'We will go talk at that table. Make sure we always have drinks.' Eileen grabbed Sandra's hand and led her to the table.

The two men nervously watched while the women chatted.

. Two hours later, they returned to the bar counter.

'We will box each other topless and we will allow spectators, as long as they are truckers or their wives or girlfriends. We agree to fight five three-minute rounds and a sixth if there is no winner after five rounds. The match ends when one of us stays down for at least ten seconds, or if one of us has been knocked down three times. We will fight each other topless, but we will be wearing Jeans and boots. This is in theme with a truckers' catfight club. There is one thing we want to change though. We are happy with a fifty-fifty split in case of a draw, but if there is a winner, she should get the full take for the evening. Losers should not get paid.' Eileen said this in a way which made it clear this was not a negotiable term.

Both husbands nodded.

'Based on our preliminary schedules we will be at the same town in two-weeks. There is a truck stop with a huge lawn. Will you be ready to fight each other there?'

Both women nodded this time.

'Good, we will start selling tickets then.'

Chapter 2 – The First Event

The closer they got to fight night, the harder Sandra trained. John was getting nervous that she might get beaten up, but she did not have time for nerves. Her focus was on one thing only, getting herself ready to beat Eileen and take home the prize money, which was already over two-thousand dollars. Both were excited when the morning of their trip to the fighting venue arrived. John booked Sandra into the truck stop as soon as they arrived in the town to give her time to relax and prepare for the fight. The rest of the day seemed to slow down for him. He could no longer wait to see his wife in a topless boxing match against another tough woman. But the hours felt like days. He was exhausted when he finally joined her at the truck stop. It was only six in the evening, meaning he had to wait another six hours for the fight. They had a light early dinner. Afterwards, they rested in their room until it was time for the fighters to be introduced to the spectators. Dave had come up with this idea. He was sure that this would convince any truckers in the pub, who did not have tickets, to buy some. Sandra put on her jeans, boots and bikini top. She covered her upper body with a leather jacket. When they arrived at the pub, Dave and Eileen were waiting for them. It surprised John how many women were in the pub. He expected mainly men.

Dave bought four shooters and lifted his glass. 'To a good fight.'

'To a good fight,' repeated the other before downing the shooter.

'Ladies and gentlemen. It is time to introduce you to our fighters. If you do not have tickets yet, please buy them as soon as possible. There is only space for a limited number of spectators. Now, ladies and gentlemen, please welcome our first fighter, Eileen from Wichita, Kansas.'

Eileen took off her leather jacket and left it on the bar counter. Her red bikini top showed off plenty of her slightly sagging D-cup breasts. She walked confidently through the crowd and stood next to Dave.

When the cheers and wolf whistles died down, Dave continued. 'Her opponent from Fish Creek, Wisconsin, Sandra.'

Sandra left her leather jacket with John. Her black bikini top also showed off ample amounts of her firm D-cup breasts. Like her opponent, she confidently made her way through the crowd and took her place on the other side of Dave.

When the crowd settled down, Dave continued. 'Ladies and gentlemen. These two lovely ladies will box each other topless in just under three hours. It will be a debut for both of them. Each of these ladies is so confident she would beat the other up, they agreed on a winner-takes-all arrangement for the prize money. The loser goes home with nothing but bruises.' Dave waited again for the cheers to subside. 'If you still don't have a ticket, make your way to John at the bar counter. But hurry. He only has a few tickets left. You will never again see entertainment like this at only fifty dollars per person. If you are not convinced yet, let me introduce you to our lovely ring girl, Ruby. The sexy stripper was wearing only a short skirt and tiny pasties, only barely covering her nipples. 'If you want to see what is under those bikini tops and these pasties, be sure you have a ticket for midnight on the big lawn.'

Dave's plan worked. In the next few minutes, they sold another twelve tickets, bringing the prize money to a whopping two-thousand-seven-hundred-and-fifty dollars.

As agreed beforehand, the two fighters and their ring girl mingled with the crowd until eleven. They then went back to their rooms to warm up, lace up and get mentally prepared for their fight.

John and Sandra left their room a few minutes before twelve. When they arrived at the fighting arena, the fifty-five spectators had already formed a human boxing ring on three sides of the fighting area. They left the fourth side open for the truck lights to illuminate the arena and as an entrance to the grassy area for the fighters, seconds, referee and ring girl. Dave and Eileen arrived about a minute later. Both ladies removed their leather jackets before entering the makeshift ring. This time, bikini tops did not cover their breasts. The cold air and the adrenalin rushing through their veins made their nipples as stiff as they've ever been.

The two women stared at each other from across the ring. Both had beautifully toned bodies with feminine muscles. Both had long hair tied in ponytails. Sandra's hair was red and Eileen's blonde. The redhead had green eyes, while the blonde had blue eyes. Both had pretty faces. Eileen had Barbie doll looks, while Sandra was the typical beautiful girl next door. Their D-cup breasts and stiff pink nipples looked magnificent in the headlights of the trucks. Both had flat tummies with nicely defined stomach muscles. Eileen had shapely legs and a tight bum, while the redhead sported athletic legs and a tight bum.

The buzz in the crowd increased when the referee entered the ring, followed by his now topless wife, holding a sign with a hand-written number 1 on it. Ruby slowly walked around the ring, enjoying every wolf whistle and lewd remark.

The referee waited until his wife had left the ring before he called the fighters to the middle. 'Ladies, break when I tell you to. Have a clean fight. Touch gloves. Go back to your corners.' He waited a few moments to ensure both fighters were ready. 'Fight.'

Sandra took in a deep breath before purposefully marching forward with her gloves held high. Any doubts she felt before the fight was now gone. All she cared about was landing that first punch. When they came into range, both fired a jab. Both made contact, but Sandra had the better of the exchange. Her jab landed on the blonde's nose, while she took the punch coming her way on her shoulder. Blood trickling from her opponent's nose gave her a boost of confidence. She quickly shot out a straight one-two, but Eileen easily danced out of range, only to step in with a beautiful right-cross to the redhead's temple. This knocked Sandra slightly off balance, but she recovered almost immediately. Both fighters danced out of range again. They measured the distance between them with a few jabs, but neither wanted to be the first to step in again. Both wanted to counterattack. The next two minutes went by with only stiff jabs landing. But all changed during the last fifteen seconds of the round. Both women stepped in and unloaded on each other. Neither defended as they tried to put the other down. Sandra landed a straight right to her opponent's face and followed this up with a left to her chin and a vicious uppercut, which almost knocked the blonde's left breast clean off of her chest. At the same time, Eileen landed a straight left, which totally flattened the redhead's right breast. A right hook then slammed it to the side of her body. Finally, another right hook busted Sandra's bottom lip. Each landed a few more hard punches before the referee ordered them to break for the end of the round.

'Come, sit down. Have a sip of water. Are you okay?' John was concerned about the punishment his wife took at the end of the round. Like most of the spectators, it surprised him that neither went down.

'My tit is burning like hell. Other than that, I am fine.'

John placed an ice bag on the battered breast before applying Vaseline to the busted lip. He was far from a trained cut man, but he managed to stop the bleeding before the second round started.

Having felt each other's power towards the end of the first round, the two women boxed from behind their jabs again, throwing only the occasional power punch. Both had moderate success, targeting mostly each other's tummies and tender breasts. But like the first round, they opened up during the last few seconds of the round. This time, Sandra landed a beautifully timed straight right to her opponent's left eye. It opened a slight cut on her cheekbone and caused the eye to swell close almost immediately. She also had success with a left hook which slammed the blonde's right breast into her left. Eileen landed an uppercut to her opponent's chin. She held back slightly as she was off balance when throwing it. If her balance had been better, the punch would have knocked the redhead down. After her own breasts were knocked into each other, she forced a straight right through her opponent's arms to flatten Sandra's left breast.

'You've done well. She is bleeding from her nose and the cut under her eye. She will probably soon struggle to see from her left eye. Keep throwing rights and try to hit her left eye again. How are you feeling?' John was more into the fight now. He did not worry about his wife's safety as much anymore, but was rather trying to advise her on how to beat up her opponent.

'The bitch got my right breast this time. I can't tell you how much that hurts.'

'You landed harder punches to her tits. I am sure she hurts even more. Target them as well. Left eye and tits.'

The third round started faster than the previous two. Sandra wanted to hurt her opponent early, focussing on closing her left eye and when the blonde's arms lifted to protect her eye, sneaking an uppercut into her boobs. These tactics worked well for her. Eileen was too busy protecting her swollen eye and bruised boobs to mount her own attack. She landed mostly jabs, but nothing which could hurt her opponent. But the blonde once again woke up towards the end of the round. After taking two more punches to her left eye, it was almost completely swollen closed now. Her breasts had been battered about like pinballs and were burning like an open flame. She knew she had taken too much punishment during the round and hoped for a flash knockdown. She almost got it just before the referee stopped the round.

Sandra threw a left uppercut to her breasts, and she caught the redhead with a short right to the temple. The older woman stumbled backwards and just managed to keep her balance. If there was more time in the round, she would have been in real trouble.

'She caught you with a lucky punch at the end. You dominated the round. Look at her eye. She is now blind on her left side. Right hooks will land every time. Do you see how she is cupping her tits with her gloves? A few more hard punches to them and I think she will quit the match.'

Eileen came out swinging when the fourth round started. Dave had told her that Sandra was still feeling the effects of the near knockdown and that she should take advantage of it. But Sandra was fully recovered and alert. She easily avoided the wild punches coming her way and made her opponent pay with hard punches to her left eye and her swollen breasts. This took the wind out of the blonde. She expected to put her opponent down, but got the worst of the exchange instead. She was slightly disheartened and fell back into her tactics of covering up most of the round. But her defensive skills were not good enough, and she took lots of punishment to her left eye and breasts in particular. She once again let her fists go towards the end of the round, but this time Sandra ensured she stayed out of range.

'She will be desperate in the last round. Watch out for wild punches. Stay tight and target her left eye and breasts again. She will not last another three minutes if you stay controlled and accurate.'

John's advice was on the money. Eileen did not want to take more punishment to her eye and breasts. Her only defence was to knock her opponent out early in the round. She rushed in and feinted a punch. When Sandra stepped back to get out of range, she followed her and grabbed hold of her. The blonde pushed her opponent into the crowd and landed a few body shots. Sandra saw an uppercut coming and was about to bring her arms up to block it. But an idiot behind her tried to cop a feel at that moment. His arm blocked her and the uppercut thundered into her chin. For a split second, all went black. Luckily, the same guy stopped her from falling. Her legs were still unstable, but she saw the next punch coming and easily ducked under it, grabbing hold of the blonde's body and pushing her back to the centre of the ring. By the time the referee broke them apart, her legs were stable enough for her to dance in and out of range. Eileen was now swinging with all she had, but she could not land any power shots. To make things worse, Sandra was picking her off again. The redhead was landing almost at will. After a vicious uppercut to her left breast, the blonde lowered her arms. She did not see the right hook coming. It caught her flush on the chin. Her knees buckled, and she stumbled about, unable to find her balance. Sandra rushed in to finish her, but the referee stopped her.

'Knockdown. Her knee touched the grass.' He started counting to eight, while Dave and Eileen complained about the call.

Sandra was also upset. She was also sure that her opponent's knee never touched the ground. If the referee had not stopped her, though, she would have finished the blonde in the next few seconds. By the time the referee counted to eight, there were only a few seconds left in the fight. Eileen knew she needed at least a knockdown, but she just did not have enough energy left, so she grabbed hold of the redhead and rode out the last few seconds.

After calling the last round, the referee grabbed Sandra's wrist and lifted her hand above her head. 'The winner by one knockdown to zero, Sandra!'

The two exhausted topless boxers embraced in the middle of the ring, while the crowd went absolutely mad while showing their appreciation for a hard-fought fight. They witnessed a brutal, bloody spectacle which was also very sexy. Even the women in the crowd were hot with fight lust.

'Good fight. But my knee never touched the ground.'

'I know. I was also upset, because the referee stopped me from knocking you out. But I do not want to win this way. If you promise me another fight in about a month's time, I will split the money with you.'

'I will fight you again whether or not you split the money with me. This was the most fun I've had in a very long time.'

'Me too.'

That night, after splitting the money, the two topless boxers and their husbands had drinks in John and Sandra's room.

'I hope you guys enjoyed this. Our bodies are battered and bruised and you will not touch our breasts for a while. We may be crazy, but we decided to do this again in about a month's time.'

Moments later, there was a knock on the door. The referee opened it just enough for his head to peek through the opening. 'I apologise if I got that call wrong. But I called what I saw.'

'No worries. We came to our own arrangement. The two of us will fight again in about a month's time. Will you be the referee again?' Eileen gave him a friendly smile.

'Sure, I will love to. My wife also has something to ask you.' He fully opened the door to allow Ruby to enter the room.

'How do I join this club? I also want to box and I am not the only one. At least two other women asked me about having fights.'

'You are welcome to join the fun. We will take names and contact details of potential fighters and will inform everyone where and when the next fights will be. John was excited to have more women joining the Truckers Catfight Club as it soon became known as.

The next event saw three topless fights between six women, including a rematch between Sandra and Eileen. This time, Sandra won without any controversy. Ruby had a bad-tempered fight against another stripper, who was also the wife of a trucker. They almost got into a fistfight after their match, but a promise of a rematch calmed them down enough to refrain from tearing each other apart. Just over a hundred spectators watched this event. John and Dave realised this was about the capacity crowd. There was just not enough space for more. Each event had more women competing. It got to a point where they had ten-plus fights per night. But this meant that the prize money per fight significantly reduced. The two pioneer topless boxers and their husbands learned from each mistake and soon limited the fights per night to five, while also introducing three weight classes. These were not the same as those used in organised boxing and also did not share its weight class names. They were simply under 115lbs; 115 to 130 lbs and over 130 lbs.

The truck stop topless boxing events continued for years, but died down in the early nineties when both John and Dave retired from driving trucks.

Chapter 3 – Revival Plans

Lisa was a petite female truck driver. Men often underestimated her skills because of her small size. But she learned to drive from her grandfather, John and had more skills than most of the men who judged her. His business went to her father, but when he tragically died in a truck accident, John had to step back in to run the business for a while, whilst teaching his twenty-year-old granddaughter the ropes. He died two years after she took over the business, and now her grandmother, Sandra was at death's door. Lisa had been taking short hauls only to ensure she could visit the old woman every day. Most days, she would read to her grandmother, but today was different. Sandra motioned for her granddaughter to sit down on the bed next to her.

'How are you doing, my dear?'

'I am well, grandma. The business is doing very well.'

'Do you have a man yet?'

'No grandma. I do not have time for men. The business takes up most of my time and the spare time I do have I want to spend with you and my friends.'

'Your grandpa and I were best friends. We shared everything, our hopes and dreams, our joys and fears, and most importantly, our sexual fantasies.'

'Grandma!'

'Sex is a beautiful thing, my dear. We are all sexual creatures. Exploring your sexual fantasies is not only natural, but also makes life worth living. Never be scared to be open with your partner about your sexual likes and dislikes.'

'Should I not read to you?'

'No, my dear. I have something to tell you. But first, please fetch me the shoebox at the back of my cupboard.'

Lisa looked in the cupboard and retrieved the only shoebox she could see. 'This one, grandma.'

'Bring it closer, deary. My eyesight is not what it used to be.'

Lisa sat down on the bed again and handed the shoebox to the older woman. Sandra opened it and a smile came over her face. Memories flooded back into her mind. She closed the lid again before touching the younger woman's arm.

'I have never told your mother about my fighting career. But I think you need to know about it. In this box are photos and two videotapes. I want you to have these and to look at all the photos and to watch both video tapes. I want you to remember me the way I was back then, and not as the old, broken woman I am now. I want to show you a few of the photos now, but you will have to watch the videos at home. First, I need to tell you about my past, though. When we were younger, your grandpa and I regularly went to biker rallies. It was the seventies and mud wrestling was just taking off. I entered the mud wrestling contests every time we went to a rally, and I really enjoyed wrestling. But when your grandpa brought home a topless boxing video, my life changed forever. I just had to try it. He found me an opponent, and we boxed each other in front of a small crowd.'

'Topless, grandma?'

'Yes, deary. The female body is a work of art. We should not hide it away, especially not if we are as young and sexy as you are now. Anyway, I was hooked. That first boxing match was the best thing I have ever done. Our club grew fast. Soon, we had over fifty active boxers, all wives and girlfriends of truck drivers. We continued boxing from the late seventies to the early nineties. Unfortunately, the club then died down. Deary, there should also be a large envelope in my closet. Please bring it.'

Lisa felt uneasy talking to her grandmother about sex and topless boxing, so she grabbed the opportunity to get away from the bed for a moment, just to get her mind around what she just learned about the older woman's past.

'Shall I make us some tea, Grandma?'

'That would be lovely, deary. But please remember to bring the envelope on your way back.'

Lisa's mind was racing while making the tea in the little kitchen close to her grandmother's room. *What the hell? Grandma mud wrestling and boxing topless in front of a crowd? How can such a sweet old lady have such a wild past? She might be mixing stuff up. Maybe she and grandpa watched a few risky videos, and she is now mixing these memories with the memories of her own life. Maybe I should just humour her. She might be back to normal when I bring her a cup of tea.*

But Sandra had not forgotten their conversation when she returned. 'Thank you, dear. Please fetch the envelope as well.'

When Lisa returned with the envelope, the old woman placed it on the bed next to her. She took a sip of her tea before opening the lid of the shoebox again and took out a photo.

'This was me and Eileen fighting our second topless boxing match. She was my first opponent and also my second. After that, we had one or two more fights. But I also had fights against many other women.'

Lisa took the photo from her grandmother and looked at it. There, in black and white, was her topless grandmother boxing against another topless woman. Both were middle-aged and still had beautiful bodies.

'Larry only started taking photos from our second event, and he started making videos from about our ninth or tenth event. It is a pity I do not have photos of the first time I boxed another woman. It was probably the day I have learned the most about myself. Fighting another woman is so exhilarating. I felt invincible after the fight and I knew nothing could stop me from reaching my dreams. I was floating on air for a few days and sex with your grandfather felt better than ever. He was so horny, he could not leave me alone. I was horny too, but my breasts were in so much pain. Eileen landed a few good punches right to my breasts, but I landed a lot more to hers.'

'Grandma! I don't want to imagine you and grandpa having sex.'

'Oh, deary. We were not old and all crumpled up back then. I was still beautiful. Just look at the photo. And your grandfather was such a handsome man.'

Sandra handed her granddaughter more photos and told the story of each of them. Most were of her in action against another topless woman, but some were taken in her corner between rounds, or showing the jubilation of a win or the disappointment of a loss after a fight. Lisa could not help but to enjoy the photos. Admiration for her grandmother replaced her initial awkwardness. The old women really had a full life. She obviously enjoyed the topless boxing era of her life and she went out and did what she enjoyed, when most people probably frowned upon female boxers, let alone topless female boxers. She leaned in and kissed her grandmother on the cheek.

'You were such a sexy woman back then. I wish I had your guts to go out and do stuff. I am too scared to sing karaoke in front of other people, let alone box topless in front of a crowd. But you went out and boxed other women topless, while a crowd watched. And you did mud wrestling as well.'

'Honey, you are not even thirty yet. I started doing these things in my mid-thirties when I started feeling comfortable in my own skin. You are a beautiful young woman. Do not hide your beauty. Be proud of it. I am not saying that you should also box topless in front of a crowd. That was our thing. Female fighting turned both your grandfather and me on. I enjoyed doing it even more than I enjoyed watching it. But you must find your own joys in life. When you do, do not shy away from them because you think others may judge you. As long as you are not hurting anybody else, go out and live out your fantasies.'

'But you hurt other people, why can't I?' Lisa said this with a huge smile on her face.

'Clever, deary. We enjoyed hurting each other. We all knew what we were in for and we were all prepared to take the pain for the opportunity to have lots of fun.'

'What is in the envelope, grandma?'

The older woman picked up the envelope and handed it to her granddaughter. 'Please take good care of this. Your grandfather kept detailed notes of how he built of the Truckers Catfight Club. He noted everything that worked and every mistake he made. He also kept a log of all my fights. In here you will see dates of my fights, where we fought, my opponent's name, whether I won or lost and how I won or lost. These are very dear to me.'

'I will keep this in a safe after scanning them in, grandma.'

'You won't break them when you are scanning them?'

'No grandma. It will just save them to my computer, but nothing will happen to the pages.'

'The videos both contain some of my boxing matches. I hope you enjoy them while watching me do what I enjoyed doing most. We had a few more, but they got so worn out, we had to throw them away.'

'I will transfer these to DVD. Don't worry, I will not break the tapes. It will also keep them in my safe with the envelope and most of the photos. Will it be okay if I keep a few of these photos in my truck? I would love to get inspiration from them when I feel down. They will remind me of just how strong you were and that I could also be that strong.'

'I do not mind at all. Now read to me please, dear.'

Lisa read until her grandmother fell asleep. She gave the older woman a tender kiss on the forehead. 'I love you, grandma. You were ... are indeed a remarkable woman.'

Two days later, Sandra passed away while her granddaughter was reading to her. Lisa took a week off to arrange the funeral and to have some time to reflect. She also used this time to scan the photos and documents kept by her grandfather and to write the videos on DVDs. Late on the fourth night after her grandmother's death, she watched the first DVD. She was surprised and impressed at just how athletic and vicious her grandmother had been. She could also not believe how much punishment she had endured while boxing another strong woman. The young truck driver could not stop watching. After watching the first DVD, she made some popcorn and then watched the second. She estimated her grandmother was in her mid-fifties in the last video on the tape. She was boxing a woman in her forties and still knocked her down twice in their five-round bout.

'I wish I could look half as good and have a fraction of her guts when I turn forty, let alone fifty' she thought to herself.

Two weeks later, Lisa pulled into a truck stop, excited to meet up with three of her female friends, who were also truck drivers. Alexa and Mindi were lesbian lovers and Tessa was a single thirty-one-year-old. The four of them enjoyed each other's company and met up as often as their schedules allowed for. She saw their two trucks when she parked hers and rushed to book in so she could catch up with them in the pub, where she knew they would be. A shooter and a whisky already waited for her when she joined their table. All three of her friends hugged and kissed her.

'How are you doing?' Tessa was her closest friend.

'Much better. I miss her a lot, but I can deal with that. I just scare the hell out of motorists when they see the driver of an eighteen-wheeler crying her eyes out at sixty miles an hour.'

They all laughed at this. The conversation changed to less serious topics, and the women had a good laugh while having a few drinks.

'I have the craziest family. Does anybody else's family do stuff that is way out there?' Mindi wanted to continue with her story, but Lisa interrupted her.

'Yes, my grandmother used to mud wrestle and she also competed in topless boxing fights against wives and girlfriends of truck drivers.'

'That was a rhetorical question, honey. But my interest is piqued. Please tell more.' Mindi gave her a sweet smile.

'Oh, sorry. No, finish your story.'

'It is boring. My overweight, lazy, fifty-year-old-uncle is sure he will be able to run the Boston marathon this year. He is out of breath each time he goes to the fridge to stuff his body with more junk food. There you have it. Now, back to your story. Your grandma was a topless boxer?'

'Yes, when she was in her forties and early fifties, she boxed topless for a club started by my grandfather and his friend Dave. Her first two fights were against Dave's wife, Eileen. I knew all these people.'

'Kudos for her. You say they had a club?'

'Yes, it was only for wives and girlfriends of truckers. Back then, there were not really female truckers.'

'How did it work? Where did they fight?'

'The wives and girlfriends let my grandfather know when they wanted to box. He then looked who would be in the same area on a specific date and organised an event at one of the truck stops. They used trucks to make a square. The spectators would line up against the trucks on three sides and the women would box in the fighting area they created. They had over fifty female fighters and divided them into three weight classes. He limited the fights per event to five and the spectators to a hundred. The fighters then shared the prize money collected from the tickets sold. For most fights, the winner would get seventy percent and the loser thirty percent of the money allocated to the fight. But some fighters preferred to fight under winner-gets-all rules. The allocation gets complicated. My grandfather divided the total take between the five fights. But the higher the fighters in a fight were ranked, the bigger cut that fight got from the take.'

'I wish I could see something like that.' Alexa was quiet until now. She did not try to hide the lust in her voice.

'I have two DVDs with some of my grandma's fights.'

'What are we waiting for? Off to your room.'

After settling their bill, the four women rushed to Lisa's room. She put the first DVD in her laptop and opened the first fight. The other three watched in silence, but Alexa was cheering the fighters on.

'That's it. Hit her in the tits.'

'Stop cheering for my grandma's opponent.'

'Sorry, I just want to see them hit the shit out of each other.'

'Your grandma was so sexy. We should totally do something like this.'

Tessa looked serious.

'Fight each other?' It surprised Lisa that her best friend would suggest something like that.

'Yes. But also start the club again.'

'That is a great idea. Mindi and I will beat each other up. We frustrate each other often enough, so a good fight may just be what we need to sort out our shit. The two of you are also perfect opponents for each other. You are such tiny little things. It will be so cute when you beat each other up.' Alexa was fully into this idea.

'Your tits are so small, I will have to be very accurate to hit them.' Tessa flicked her best friend's right breast with the back of her hand.

'Fuck you, bitch. You also have B-cups.'

The two petite friends playfully wrestled each other for a few seconds, each trying to give the other's breasts a playful squeeze.

'The battle of the tiny tits. I can see the headlines.' Mindi pressed her chest forward to show how much bigger her D-cups were.

'Is it settled then? Are we doing this?' Alexa truly wanted to fight her lover and she also wanted to watch other topless women fight each other.

'I will think about it.' Lisa was not sure yet.

'I am in' said Tessa and Mindi in unison.

'Okay, peer pressure got me again. I will start planning. Next time we see each other, we will finalise the plans and arrange the first event. Are we all fighting in it?'

'Yes,' they all agreed.

'How are we going to get the word out?' Tessa wanted to fight, but she also wanted to make sure she made money from her fight.

'I think we should put flyers at truck stops, but I also want to talk to a few old-timers who may have attended some of the events in the 1990's before the club died down.'

The women were too excited to sleep, so they all chatted for another few hours. All had to stay over an extra day at the truck stop to comply with their sleeping quota, but they didn't mind. All felt positive they were onto something big.

Chapter 4 – Club Rules

Over the next few days, Lisa thought about the conversation she and her three friends had about reviving the topless boxing club. She used every opportunity she had to put ideas on paper, using her grandfather's notes and some of her own ideas. When she had the basics down, she organised with her three friends to meet her at a truck stop a few days later. That night, while going to the pub of the truck stop where she was overnighting, she saw two old-timers chatting with each other. She had previously asked one of them, called Mike, for advice, and he had been very helpful. At least she knew he was not part of the 'men-only' club. She had gotten so many sexist answers when trying to get advice from some men. There had been so many instances that she could not even recall all. But some of her favourites were:

'Honey, rather go find you a husband who can support your cute little ass. Trucking is not for pretty little dolls like you.'

'You need a tip? If you have to ask, trucking is not for you. But I will tip you if you dance for me nicely.'

'You try to take our jobs and now you expect me to help you do it. Leave this man's job to the men, sweet cheeks.'

But most men were quick to give other men advice. Nobody could make it as a trucker without learning from those who had been in the game longer than them. But at least one of these old-timers was not like that. He was kind and did not get upset when she did not immediately get his advice and had to ask again. She motioned for the bar lady and took a seat next to

Mike.

'May I buy you gentlemen a round to say thank you for all the times you've helped me?'

'I will never say no to a pretty lady like you. Lisa, is it? This is my friend, Ant.'

'Yes, Lisa. Hi, Ant.' Lisa shook the older man's hand. 'Mike here has given me good advice in the past, and I hope to get some advice again. But this time, not about trucking.'

'Don't ask him about computers or women. He knows even less about these than I do.'

'Maybe I can help you with both of those,' said Lisa while grinning at Ant's dry humour.

'Don't bother. Only fools and young men try to understand women. At our age, we understand that women are not to be understood. Maybe you can show us one day how to find all this porn they are talking about on our computers.'

Lisa laughed before paying for the three beers. The bar lady probably assumed she wanted the same as the two men.

'Cheers. Thank you for the drink.'

'Cheers, honey. I am not sure my advice was worth a beer, but I will take it.'

'Cheers. Your advice was priceless. I recently learned about a topless boxing club, where wives and girlfriends of truckers used to box at truck stops. Have either of you ever been to any of these events?'

This got the attention of both older men.

'Ant and I were talking about those days just the other night. Those women were not only fun to look at, they could really box. Their skills put many a man to shame. Back then, guys were too proud to admit they enjoyed the boxing skills as well. All pretended they were only watching to see them titties fly all over the place. Where did you hear about it?'

'My grandfather and his friend started the club. Their wives were the first two women to have a topless boxing match for the club.'

'Are you John or Dave's granddaughter?'

'John's'

'How is Sandra? She was one of the kindest women I've known, but she was a wild woman while boxing.'

'She died recently. But before she did, she told me about the club and she gave me a few videos, photos and notes my grandpa made about the club.'

'I am so sorry for your loss.'

'Thank you.'

'I am also sorry. Your grandmother was a remarkable woman. She and the other boxers showed many of us that women could do anything. It made it easier for us to accept when women started driving trucks.'

'Thank you. Many men still don't like female drivers.'

'Them arseholes should have watched more female boxing.'

'You wanted to ask us for advice about the boxing club?' Mike hoped to talk about it some more with the beautiful young female driver.

'Yes. Three other female drivers and I are talking about starting up the club again. Do you think drivers will support it and do you have any advice?'

'Tits will always bring men. But they may get bored with it and choose to rather watch a strip show if the women fighting do not have skills. Most of us prefer a good contest. Foxy boxing is fun to watch for a while. Seeing tits jiggle and bounce is always fun. But we can watch them do that while drinking at the pub at almost any truck stop. There is always a pretty lady willing to take her clothes off to music.' Mike motioned with his eyes towards two young women sitting at a table. Like most truck stops, this one had a few stay-in strippers to entertain the truckers.

'I did not think of that. We will have to get some training before having our first event. How many fights do you think we should have during each event?'

'There used to be around five or six. That seems about right, but please don't do it so late at night. We all need to book our sleeping hours. Nobody can stay up until three in the morning to watch women slug it out.'

'At the moment, we only have two fights for the first event. We will look for more fighters, though.'

'Two fights might be enough for the first event. But perhaps try to get at least one more fight.'

'We are still feeling our way through this. We will approach a few other female drivers we know, but we do not have a proper plan yet on how to convince other women to box each other topless while male drivers watch them. I know the prize money will help, but we probably need other incentives as well.'

'Many women enjoy fighting and the original club gave them an opportunity to do so. If you start this, women will join. Also, women are very competitive creatures. If you get positive attention, some women will join your club to share in that attention. Others will be mad at you because their husbands enjoy watching you fight. They will join for the opportunity to knock your head off.'

'And you say you do not understand women?' Lisa said this with a huge grin on her face. She knew assuming that women craved the attention of men, or would get jealous and fight when another woman got attention, was a very simplistic view on women. But she also knew this would be true of some women and that some might join for these reasons. However, she was more interested in women joining because they enjoyed fighting. She continued sitting with the two old men, telling them more about her plans and watching a few strip shows with them. Like many women, she appreciated the beauty of a semi-naked female body, especially if it was moving seductively to the beat of a good song.

When the four women met a few days later at a truck stop, Lisa had already typed up a draft set of rules. 'I would love to go through these and sign off on the rules today. The first one, do we all agree that only female truckers and wives and girlfriends of male truckers may fight for the club?'

'Yes, this is a trucker's fight club. It should be only for the trucker community.' This was something Alexa felt strongly about, and the other two also nodded their heads.

'Good. Do we all agree with five rounds of three minutes each, and a sixth if needed? Personally, I think we should drop the sixth round. If it's a draw after five, it should be a draw.'

'I kind of like the sixth round. It gives the fighters another chance to win,' said Tessa.

'I have a totally different take on this. I agree with only five rounds, but I think we should change to style of fighting. Instead of boxing gloves, I think we should use MMA gloves. Maybe we should also allow elbow and knee strikes. I thought about kicks also, but I quite like the idea of fighting in jeans and boots, so I don't think kicking each other with boots on is such a good idea.'

'That covers a few rules, Alexa. Maybe we should deal with one at a time.'

'We can, but these are all linked. If we go with traditional topless boxing, I think an extra round is a good idea. But if we change the fighting rules slightly, I think an extra round will be too much.'

'Point taken. I like the MMA gloves. But elbows and knees sound dangerous.'

'I have been to a gym yesterday. I saw two women spar against each other. They were striking with their fists, elbows, knees and feet. I could not take my eyes off of them. Imagine how captivated men would be if we allow fists, elbows and knees while fighting each other topless.'

'I like that,' said Mindi.

'So do I. Five rounds is also good then.'

It was three to one on the striking rules. 'I will change the rules. But what about injuries? How do we keep everybody safe?'

'We need medics anyway, even if we only box each other. This is not the seventies anymore. There will be risks for us when we fight, so we need somebody with medical knowledge to be ringside. I suggest we have at least two medics every event and that we have back-up drivers just in case a fighter cannot deliver her haul after the fights.' It was clear Alexa had done her homework.

'Have we bitten off more than we can chew?' Lisa felt slightly overwhelmed.

'No, we can do this. We will never get licenses for this, so it will be underground fights. But I think the spectators will enjoy it more because of that. Logic dictates that we will have broken noses, ribs and maybe more. The fighters all will have to sign a release. We will have to keep a fund to help pay for medical bills. I know I am jumping ahead again, but I suggest only fifty percent of the take should go towards prize-money. Twenty-five percent should go into this medical fund, and the rest to cover expenses like medics, lawyers, referees and ring girls. If we do this right, the fifty percent would still allow for a significant amount for each fighter. We can charge high gate fees once truckers know they will see great fights between topless women.'

'I agree with Alexa. She has obviously thought about this a lot. I nominate her as the chairperson of the club.' It was difficult for Lisa to give up power. But she really wanted the new club to be successful, and she knew her friend was better suited to run it than she was.

'I agree.'

'So do I.'

'I got a few ideas from a few old-timers, though. They think we should have the fights earlier in the evening so that all the fighters and spectators could still book enough sleeping hours. They also think we should all have training before we fight. Men want to watch a good fight. Breasts will only keep them coming for so long. They can see those at the strip shows inside the truck stops as well. As soon as we have our first event, they believe more women will join. They think it would be for attention or jealousy, but I hope we could attract women who enjoy fighting.'

'I agree with the time. But we risk being shut down should the police find out about our events. Maybe we should only have events where the truck stop has a very private parking area. I can think of at least five, but I am sure we will find more. If we do it away from prying eyes, we can probably start the event at eight. A fight will last at most just over twenty minutes, including its breaks between rounds. If we allow thirty minutes, the five fights will be over in about two-and-a-half hours. Let's add another thirty minutes for unforeseen delays. This means all five fights will be done at eleven. Do we all agree on five fights when we have enough fighters?'

The other three all agreed with Alexa.

'I also agree with training. If we want to have great events, which will continue to attract spectators, we have to have fighting skills. I joined a gym-group with many branches. This means I can practice in almost any city where I haul to. I suggest you do the same. We will make it mandatory for new fighters to have at least three months' training before they have their first fight. I also think we should only have our first event in three months' time to ensure our own skills are good enough to give the spectators a show they would talk about for years. We should rather have fewer shows with fewer fights until new fighters are skilled. Do you agree?' The other women agreed with her.

'The last rule is the knockout or three knockdown rule and the most knockdowns win rule. I like these.'

The others also agreed to keep these rules.

'Excellent. Lisa, will you update the rules and send it to the rest of us? We will then have a last look at it before signing it off. Mindi and I will find a lawyer to draw up the fighter's agreements. We will also find medics for each venue where we will have our events. We will also look for MMA referees near each of our venues. With time, we will train truckers or their significant others as our own referees and maybe even as medics. Can we all look for more safe venues? I will send you a list of those I've identified. Tessa, will you then talk to the strippers at each of these venues to be our ring girls?'

All the women were excited by the progress they've made during this meeting. The fighting club now seemed like a reality and not just a pipedream.

Chapter 5 – Training

Two days after Alexa had joined a gym, Lisa joined the same gym group. That same evening, she went to their gym in the city where she had a delivery. The MMA instructor told her his next class would start in thirty minutes and that she should change and warm up. When she joined the class in very short blue shorts and a pink crop top, she expected to get into the ring for a sparring session. But instead, the instructor made her do strength exercises before allowing her to hit the heavy bag. One of his assistants helped her with her movement and balance, while the instructor was helping four pairs of women with their sparring sessions.

'When do I get to spar?'

'You are new here. Once you've mastered the basics, you will be allowed to have sessions against other women.'

'But I travel around and will go to many of your gyms.'

'Each instructor will give you a brief progress report if you ask. The next gym will then use this to decide what training plan is best for you.'

'How long will it take before I am ready to fight?'

'Do you have a fight planned?'

'No, but I want to know at what level I will be after … say, three months.' Lisa did not want to share the club's plans with the assistant.

'That depends on you. Some people are ready to make their amateur debut after training for a couple of months. Others never get to that level.'

This gave Lisa hope and motivated her to work as hard as possible. Over the next month, she made it to a gym nearly every day, taking in all that the trainers and assistants shared with her. But she wondered whether she would be one of those people who would never get to a point where she would be ready to have a fight. But when she handed her progress report to a female instructor at a gym, the women invited her onto the exercise mat.

'Let's see what you have. Fists only. Move around and punch this glove.' The instructor held the large glove she had on her left hand and allowed the young trucker to punch it before she moved and held it at a different elevation.

Lisa quickly got into it. She moved like the assistants had taught her, stepping in to land a combination before moving out again.

'Good. Now elbows only. Use your hips more. Put more weight behind your striking weapons.'

After the elbow session, the instructor picked up a thick pad and allowed her student to kick and knee it.

'Good. You are ready for your first sparring session. There are a few headgears in that cupboard. We clean them every time they are used, so don't get all girly on me about not wanting to put it on your head if others wore it. Pick one and put it on. I have another woman at your level. She is changing. As soon as she is ready, the two of you can spar for a bit.'

Lisa's sparring partner was taller than her and outweighed her by about ten pounds. But this did not bother her. All that mattered was that she was about to throw hands with another woman. When both women were ready, the instructor called them to join her on the fighting mat. 'Mary, this is Lisa.

Lisa, this is Mary.' She waited for the two nervous women to shake hands before continuing. 'Punches only until I tell you otherwise. Are you both ready? Fight.'

Both rookie fighters were slightly tentative. They moved in slowly before testing their range with a few jabs. Lisa had a reach disadvantage and ate a few jabs in the face while having no success. She realised she had to get closer to her opponent and, if she was not aggressive enough, Mary would just continue punching her in the mouth with stiff jabs. After moving out of range, she waited for her opponent to follow her before quickly closing the distance between them. Although she took another punch to the face while going in, she landed four of her own before Mary grabbed hold of her. After separating them, the instructor allowed them to spar for another minute. Both had successes and their adrenalin levels were overflowing when the instructor made them break for a rest. The next round, she allowed them to kick as well. This tipped the scale further in the taller woman's favour. Her longer legs punished the petite woman every time she tried to get close enough to land her punches. Lisa was not totally without success though. She took a lot of kicks to her body and a few punches to her face, but she also landed a few kicks to her opponent's thighs and got close enough one time to land two solid punches to her face.

After another break, the instructor allowed them to use all four of their striking weapons. Once again, Lisa found it difficult to get close enough to throw elbows and knees, but she was so eager to try these out that she was willing to take a few hard strikes on her way in. Both women were exhausted by the time the instructor called an end to the sparring session.

'Good work ladies. You've done very well for your first sparring session. You coped better than expected with being punched in the face. How do you feel?'

'This is the best thing I've ever done. I feel like I'm floating on a cloud.' Lisa was all smiles, although she had a thick lip.

'I agree. Who could imagine fighting could be this much fun?'

'Good, go shower. Mary, I will see you tomorrow. Lisa, I hope to see you again soon.'

Although they had just met, Lisa felt very close to Mary after sharing a sparring session with her and she needed to give her a hug. No words were needed. Both women felt the same. They hugged for a few seconds before heading to the change room together.

'That was so much fun. But I hate those long legs of yours. They made it so difficult for me to get close enough to land my strikes.'

'Oh, you landed enough. I am afraid my face will be all swollen up tomorrow.'

'Do you have to go to the office tomorrow? Luckily, nobody will see my face while I am driving my truck.'

'Are you a truck driver? So is my husband. And no, I do not work at the moment. We moved here recently and I am still looking for an opportunity to make some money.'

'You can make money fighting.'

'I hope so. But it takes time to become a pro. I work hard though and hope to make some money from this in the next few years. But until then, I will have to find something a bit more ladylike to earn some cash.'

'No, I mean, you can make money fighting for our club?'

'What do you mean?'

'Let's shower and get dressed. I will tell you all about it over dinner, my treat.'

'I am intrigued. How can I say no? It will haunt me forever if I do not find out more about your club.'

Later, at a seafood restaurant, Lisa told Mary all about how her grandfather started a female topless boxing club in the seventies, how her grandmother boxed for the club and how they were now reviving the club. Mary phoned her husband while they were waiting for desert to tell him she would fight for the club in a few months' time. When she returned to their table, she smiled at her new friend.

'Men! He was all concerned until I told him we will be fighting topless. Then he was suddenly very supportive. We are definitely in.'

Chapter 6 – Fight Night

Alexa quickly found an opponent for Mary. Her husband was a driver, and she travelled with him. They were both at the pub when Alexa handed out flyers advertising their first event and she immediately came up to her to find out more. Ten minutes later, she committed to fight Mary. She had been a boxer when she was younger, but was happy to adapt to the club's fighting rules. The six fighters all continued training hard until fight night arrived. Alexa had picked the venue for their first event well. It was off the main roads, but central enough for all the fighters and spectators to arrange their schedules to be near it on the day of the fights. All of them had a short drive to get there in time for the fights. The large parking area was surrounded by very high walls and two security guards, who were more than happy to make some extra cash during the event, controlled its entrance. The fights would be far away from where anybody without a ticket would be. The only downside was that there was no grass in the parking area. Most of it was covered with gravel. But Alexa found an area towards the back where the ground was free of gravel. It was slightly muddy, but not enough to make movement in it difficult. Although it was close enough to two of the walls to only park trucks and trailers on the other two sides, she decided to keep to tradition and to park trucks and trailers on those two sides as well. The hundred tickets available sold out quickly at one-hundred-and-fifty dollars a ticket, which Alexa advertised as a onetime special. She wanted to increase the price to two-hundred-and-fifty dollars as soon as they could guarantee five fights per event. This guaranteed a decent payday for each fighter, even the losers. It also started off their injury fund with a nice three-thousand dollars. After paying the two medics, the referee and the two ring girls five-hundred dollars each, they were left with two-thousand dollars. Alexa knew they had to build up a buffer for less successful events.

Lisa arrived at the truck stop early. Although she and Tessa had talked often and had shared their progress with each other, they agreed not to catch up before their fight. Neither wanted to get distracted, and neither wanted to think of her opponent as her best friend. They needed to see the other as the enemy who would destroy them if they did not destroy her first. But Lisa said hi to Alexa and Mindi, who had no qualms about beating each other up later. After chatting with them for a while, she went looking for Mary. She and her husband were at the pub, getting some liquid courage into her.

'Would you mind if I join you?'

'Hi Lisa!' Mary was already slightly loud as the alcohol had taken effect. 'Bobby, this is the woman I have told you about. Lisa, this is my husband, the booby lover.'

Lisa smiled while Bobby just shook his head at his wife's comment. They shook hands before Bobby excused himself to go to the bathroom.

'You have to slow down. It will be a tough fight tonight. You can't afford to be off balance.'

'I am so nervous, though.'

'So am I. I am fighting one of my best friends.'

'Help me with this shot, then.' Mary was double parked and handed one to her former sparring partner.'

'I will if you promise this is the last one before your fight.'

'Very well, spoilsport.'

They downed the shot, and Mary immediately ordered two more.

'Mary. You promised.'

'I know, but you need another, and I can't let you drink on your own.'

'Okay, but this is my last and yours too.'

'Don't worry about her. She will be ready to fight. She is a nervous drinker, but she will not disappoint you in the fighting pit. My girl always rocks up when it is time to go.' Bobby sat down again.

'Have you been in fights, then?'

'No, she is just an all-round sport star. We've had some big nights and she would be the best player the next day, no matter what sport she was competing in.'

'Excuse my husband, the thought of seeing topless fights later is clouding his mind. I love sport, but I am not nearly as good as he makes me sound.'

'Oh, she is just modest. You will see tonight.'

The three of them chatted for a few more minutes before Lisa excused herself to go get ready for her fight. The closer it got to her fight, the more nervous she became. She wondered whether it was a good idea to fight her closest friend. Her grandmother had boxed her friend, but they only really became good friends after their fight. Her two lesbian friends were different. They always had a go at each other. If you didn't know them, you would sometimes think they were enemies. But they truly loved each other and their fight would definitely settle a few brewing issues between them.

All who really knew them were confident they needed a good punch-up. But all also knew this would never change how they felt about each other. But Lisa and Tessa had no issues with each other. Their friendship was almost perfect. What if fighting each other resulted in bad blood between them? Lisa knew she had to trust her friend and herself, but she was still nervous.

Although the fighting pit was only five minutes from her room and although she was supposed to only be there just before eight, the young trucker could no longer wait and left for the fighting pit at a quarter to eight. She could hear the excitement of the crowd as she approached. Alexa was telling them about the fighters and the rules.

'Ladies and gentlemen, we have one of our atomweight fighters approaching. Please welcome Lisa.' Alexa was surprised at how early Lisa was, but she wanted her to be hyped up by the crowd.

The cheers and wolf whistles brought a smile to Lisa's face, especially because most of the wolf whistles came from other women. They seemed to be almost more excited to see the fights than the men were. Some men were probably only at the fights to see naked breasts flying about and being punched every so often. But most of the women in the audience wanted to experience a female fight. Some were thinking about joining the club, but wanted to get a feel for it first.

But one woman, Amanda, was there to get ammunition against the four female truck drivers who started the club. To be fair, she was not on her own. Her husband, Thomas, stood behind her, looking at the tiny female fighter with disgust in his eyes.

The rest of the crowd continued cheering until the little redhead entered the fighting area. Once she did, the volume almost doubled when she casually took off her leather jacket and threw it aside. It was a lovely night, and the walk made her hot. But the main reason she did this was to get the awkwardness of going topless in front of other drivers, out of the way.

The crowd loved what they saw. The petite redhead had a very sexy body and a beautiful face. Her short red hair was always perfectly styled. She had high cheekbones, a small nose and a small mouth. But the most striking facial feature was her intelligent green eyes. Many men were staring at them instead of her perky B-cup breasts and stiff pink nipples. Her tummy was flat and all the hard work in the gym over the past three months gave her a well-defined sixpack. The jeans she was wearing were tight and showed off her tight little bum and her shapely thighs. To keep warmed-up, the sexy fighter shadow boxed, throwing a few elbows and knees between the fast punches. The volume of the cheering increased even more.

Back in her room, which was close to the parking area, Tessa could hear the commotion. She could no longer wait. Her nerves were killing her, and she needed to fight before she talked herself out of it. In her rush, she completely forgot to cover her naked torso with a leather jacket. The crowd started cheering for her even before Alexa could alert them to her presence. Men have a sixth sense for bare breasts and they sensed a beautiful pair of B-cups with long, dark nipples approaching.

It was difficult to decide which of the opponents were sexier. The blue-eyed blonde had a petite nose and full lips, covered with red lipstick. The rest of her war paint on her face was subtle, but highlighted her piercing blue eyes and her high cheekbones. Like her rival, she was wearing a jean which clung to her tight bum and athletic legs. Sweat and tears at the gym also gave her a flat tummy with a nice sixpack.

'Ladies and gentlemen. We have about eight minutes before our first fight of the night, an atomweight bout between the twenty-nine-year-old Lisa and the thirty-one-year-old Tessa. Both stand five-feet-two-inches tall. Lisa hits the scales at a-hundred-and-four pounds, while Tessa outweighs her by one pound. These ladies have been training hard over the past three months to punch each other in the face. These two are best friends and a lot of pride is at stake.'

The atmosphere around the fighting pit was palpable. But this did not change Amanda's and Thomas' views. Their religious views were extreme. Although Amanda was always on the road with her husband, they both believed women should not do a man's job. It was bad enough that these women were driving trucks, but now they were making a mockery of everything sacred by fighting each other while being half naked.

Both women were shadow boxing in their corners in the bright lights of the three trucks facing the arena to illuminate the fighting area. Watching these two sexy women shadow boxing topless, was almost worth the price of admission. But the crowd was in for much more than they expected. Most thought this would be foxy boxing where the women did not really know how to punch. But these women took the fights seriously and were well prepared to beat each other up.

Lisa was completely focussed when the referee called them to the centre of the muddy fighting pit. Any doubts about beating her best friend up had left her mind. All she could think of now was to win this fight.

'Ladies, do you want to touch gloves?'

The two petite fighters went one better. They gave each other a tight hug before separating with their gloves up, ready to fight.

'Touching titties is even better.' Alexa, who was in Lisa's corner, said this loud enough to get another loud cheer from the crowd. The two fighters and their two corner women knew tight hugs or breast bumps was a good idea for all future fights.

'Ladies, back to your corners. Come out fighting.' The referee waited for both small fighters to get to their corners. 'Lisa, are you ready? Tessa, are you ready? Fight!'

The two light fighters easily glided over the thin layer of mud, touching a high glove before having at each other. Their punches were lightning fast, with lots of sting to them. Both landed, but their energetic movement kept them mostly out of harm's way. Most of the punches finding their target were to the body. After a direct punch flattened her left breasts, Lisa went tit-hunting. She wanted to inflict the same burning pain on her friend's breasts. But this distracted her and her defence suffered for it. Although she landed a beautiful uppercut which walloped the blonde's right breasts upwards, she paid for this with a thunderous right hook smashing into her chin moments later. Her lights went out, and she found herself face-down in the mud. The redhead regained her senses and was back to her feet, within four counts. Tessa impatiently waited out the eight-count, raring to go after her friend again. She had her in trouble and could smell victory.

Lisa was also eager to start again. Getting dropped embarrassed her, and she wanted to retaliate. Although she felt slightly groggy, she floated forward as soon as the referee instructed them to fight again. They met each other with a flurry of punches. Both landed, and Lisa only stayed on her feet by grabbing hold of her opponent's neck. Training kicked in, and she landed two fast knees to the blonde's ribs. This forced Tessa to tie up as well. Both gripped the other's neck tightly, while throwing more knees to each other's sides. Some of these connected, but these lacked power as their bodies were too close together and their skills were not yet at a level where they could generate enough power from this position.

Both soon realised they were not punishing the other. When they broke, Lisa landed a short, but brutal, elbow to the blonde's left eye. This put her on her bum, while blood dripped from the cut above her eye. The blue-eyed woman was only slightly stunned and was mad at herself for going down. She, now more than ever before, wanted to take her friend's head off, but the round ended before the eight count was done.

The two petite fighters glared at each other from across the fighting pit. Both had felt the other's power, and both were mad about going down. Lisa did not hear a word Alexa said. Instead, she focussed on doing damage to her friend. Tessa allowed Mindi to stop the blood from the cut above her eye. But she was also not listening to her. Clever fighting was not what she wanted to do. She wanted to hurt her friend with power strikes.

When the next round started, the crowd sensed that the intensity went up a few levels. The two topless fighters moved slower and more deliberately. They planted their feet in the thin layer of mud and threw their strikes with all the power they could muster. Both took clean punches to the face and to their breasts, but neither budged. Lisa also landed a couple of powerful elbows to the blonde's face, reopening the cut above her left eye and almost completely closing the eye. Tessa was successful with stinging knee strikes to the redhead's ribs, leaving them bruised when the round ended. The crowd was silent for a few seconds, trying to figure out how these two petite firecrackers were still on their feet before they cheered the two brawlers to their corners.

'Okay. You got that out of your system. Listen to me now. Jab until you see a gap. Go in fast, throw a few strikes and move out. Soften her up before going in for the kill.' Alexa shook her fighter by the shoulders to get her attention. But the little redhead was soon focused on her opponent again. The advice in the other corner was similar in content, but also fell on deaf ears.

When the round started, the fighters went back to the previous round's tactics. Both were taking heavy punishment in order to punish her friend. Pride was ruling their minds. Neither could live with the thought of losing to her best friend. Tessa could hardly see from her left eye and caught many punches to the left side of her face. Blood was now dripping continuously from the cut. Her own punches were landing as well, and Lisa's bottom lip was soon busted and a haematoma was forming on her forehead. But Tessa knew she was taking the brunt of the punishment, so she stepped in, grabbing her friend around the neck, pulling her head downwards. Two hard knees to her ribs made the redhead wince in pain. A third to her chin put her down again. This time she barely made it to her feet to beat the ten-count. Tessa was relentless. She threw knees and elbows, while trapping her opponent against the crowd. The people behind her stopped Lisa from falling back at least once, and she barely survived until the end of the round.

'Do you want to continue? There is no shame is stopping. You took a terrible beating.' Alexa helped her friend back to the corner.

'I will never quit. That bitch will be sorry for being in the pit with me.'

'Okay, but you have to be clever. She will be all over you. Tie her up and take some time to recover. This will frustrate her and force her to make mistakes. Only go for power punches when you see a clear opening.' Alexa was almost pleading with her fighter, while wiping the blood from her lip and icing her forehead.

'Go out and finish her. You only need one more knockdown. She has nothing left. Your knees are destroying her. A few more hard knees and she will be gone.' Mindi was much more upbeat with her fighter.

The crowd roared when both fighters answered the bell. Most of the spectators had been sure Lisa would quit between rounds. They respected her grid, but feared for her safety. She had been almost defenceless at the end of the third round and was badly beaten up. Tessa did not see a friend slowly moving towards her. All she saw was an enemy she had to destroy.

She rushed forward, throwing as she got within range. Her first punch connected with the redhead's bruised left breast, but her second missed her head by millimetres. Lisa immediately grabbed hold of the blonde, pulling her in close and pancaking their firm breasts into each other. When Tessa tried to pull away forcefully, their feet got tangled up, making them slam down into the mud. The thin layer of mud covering their upper bodies made them even sexier than before. The crowd appreciated this, while getting slightly frustrated with the lack of action. Lisa repeated this tactic about six or seven times during the round, tying her opponent up whenever she could. They tumbled down into the mud twice more, frustrating the crowd and the blonde. With about thirty seconds of the round left, Lisa had taken very little punishment and had regained her senses, but she did not show this to her opponent. Instead, she looked unstable on her feet when Tessa rushed her again. But she planted her feet just in time and threw a right elbow with all she had. The timing and aim were perfect. The referee did not even start a count, as the blonde was out cold, lying face down in the mud. No one in the crowd could believe what they had just seen. The redhead looked out on her feet, but suddenly sprung back to life, landing a devastating elbow.

Lisa immediately felt concern for her best friend. She knew just how hard that strike had been. But Tessa soon stirred, having no idea what happened to her. Mindi and Lisa helped her back to her stool, where the medics checked her out. After tending to both fighter's cuts, they decided to observe them both and decide on whether they should go to the nearest hospital, only when all the fights were done. The crowd cheered when Tessa got back to her feet, still slightly unstable. The two friends hugged for a long time in the middle of the fighting pit.

'I never want to fight you again. I love you too much.' Lisa gently kissed her friend's swollen eye.

'Don't chicken out now. I want my revenge.'

'Look at us. We both took a pretty good beating. I think you had premature revenge in the third round.'

'Fine, but you owe me for taking away an opportunity to knock you out as well.'

'Okay, I owe you one. But only if you admit I am the baddest bitch alive.'

They hugged tighter while smiling. The tight hug hurt Lisa's ribs a lot, but it was all worth it.

There was a fifteen-minute break to allow Lisa and Tessa to recover enough to act as seconds for the next fight. Although there were other women who could stand in, the two tiny fighters wanted to be involved and insisted on being in the corners. Alexa and Mindi went to the open side of the square to warm up, making sure they were not between the truck lights and the fighting pit. The crowd enjoyed this show until the next two fighters made their way to the fighting pit. Both had their leather jackets on and only removed these when Lisa called them to the centre of the fighting pit.

'Ladies and gentlemen, our next fight is in the strawweight division between Mary and Ellen. They are both five-feet-four-inches tall. Mary weighs a-hundred-and-fifteen pounds and Ellen a-hundred-and-fourteen. This is their debuts at our club.'

Mary showed no effect from the shooters she had been downing earlier. As promised, she was a wildcat in the fighting pit, taking her opponent apart. Ellen was a game opponent and landed some good strikes, but there would always be just one winner. The topless fighter sank to her knees late in the third round after a vicious knee thundered into her solar plexus. Her body was bruised and battered and her face had several cuts. But her C-cup breasts were probably her most damaged body parts. They had swollen to almost D-cup from all the punishment they took. Mary had been relentless and punished them almost at will. It impressed Lisa. Her former sparring partner indeed knew how to bring it, even after downing a bunch of shooters. The redhead looked at the crowd and smiled to herself. The event was already a big success and the two lesbian lovers still had to slug it out.

Chapter 7 – Lesbian Lovers Fight

The buzz in the crowd was electric. Nobody expected fights of this quality. They were hoping for some sexy fun, but were rewarded with two sexy, skilled and very competitive fights. Lisa enjoyed the atmosphere for a few moments. She knew that one more good fight would guarantee a sold-out show with their next event. Based on what her grandfather had written about his experiences, she also hoped this would convince more women to join their club as fighters. She looked at the sea of smiling faces, but also noticed the disgust on the faces of Amanda and Thomas. The redhead wondered why this couple in their early forties was even there. They obviously did not approve of female fighting. Why then come to a topless female fighting event? It just seemed silly to her. She could not understand the mind of a religious extremist. They were brainwashed so much, they were convinced their views were the only correct and reasonable views. This meant they would do almost anything to force others to share their extremist beliefs. And those who were not willing to change their ways had to be punished. Lisa shook her head slightly before looking over at where her two friends were warming up. Both gave her a slight nod when she made eye contact with them. It was time for the last fight of the night.

'Ladies and gentlemen. Our last fight of the evening is in the bantamweight division. This is a very special fight between two lesbian lovers who share the cab of their truck each day.'

'They will burn in hell.' The cheer from the rest of the crowd mostly drowned Amanda out. But Lisa heard it and decided not to let it go.

'They might, but not because they are lesbians or topless fighters. But judging others might also buy you a ticket straight to hell.'

This brought an even louder cheer from the crowd. Many of them were also fed-up with the negative remarks these two had been making all night. Two trucker brothers grabbed Anthony by the arms and dragged him out of the fighting arena, while their wives did the same with Amanda. The two religious extremists screamed threats at Lisa until the guards at the gate took them back to their room.

'Now that we have dealt with particular bit of fun, let's get back to the real reason we are here. Our first fighter, standing five-foot-eight-inches and weighing in at a-hundred-and-thirty-one pounds, the chairperson of the Female Truckers Fight Club, Alexa!'

The brunette jogged to the fighting pit, making her firm D-cups bounce and jiggle, while her long brown nipples grew even stiffer.

'Her opponent, standing five-foot-seven-inches and weighing in at a-hundred-and-thirty-three pounds, her lover and co-driver, Mindi!'

The blonde also jogged to the fighting pit. Her D-cups were not as firm and bounced and jiggled even more, while her thick brown nipples also stood to attention.

Lisa looked at the two twenty-seven-year-old lesbian lovers. Both had girl-next-door looks, with pretty faces, but not beauty-queen pretty. They were in good shape, but both carried a little excess weight around their hips and tummies. Their legs were sturdy and their bums firm, but full. Both had long hair tied in a ponytail. Their bodies were nicely tanned, with no tan lines.

'We do not want the three-knockdown rule. We will fight five rounds or until one of us is knocked-out.' Mindi said this without breaking eye contact with her lover.

'Ladies and gentlemen. The fighters have agreed to change the rules slightly. They will fight the full five rounds, or to a knockout. The fight will therefore not end when one of them has been knocked down three times.'

Although this was not a major rule change, the crowd cheered as if this would enhance the entertainment value of the fight exponentially.

'Ladies, please touch tits.' Lisa borrowed this expression from Alexa. The crowd once again showed their appreciation for this sexy move with a loud cheer.

The two lovers hugged each other tightly and gave each other a passionate kiss before separating. They loved each other deeply, but for the next twenty minutes, they would be competitors, each trying to knock the other one's ass the fuck out. Lisa smiled before leaving the fighting pit to give the referee control over proceedings.

'Ready? Fight!'

The crowd fell silent when the loud thuds of fists violently meeting flesh reverberated through the makeshift arena. The two lesbian lovers were not holding back. Their punches carried much more power than the fighters in the previous two fights could muster. Both immediately targeted the other's large breasts, knowing just how sensitive they were. But they also landed punches to each other's faces, ribs and tummies, while throwing the occasional knee into each other's bodies. Neither fighter moved an inch backwards. They planted their feet while they tried to demolish each other's beautiful bodies and faces. It was almost a minute into the fight before Alexa took a few steps backwards from a solid elbow to her forehead. Mindi did not follow the brunette. Instead, she used the break in action to suck in much needed air and to regain her composure. When Alexa regained her balance, she slowly moved back towards her lover. Although her arms were already feeling the strain, she once again threw punches into the blonde's body and face.. Her own body also got pummelled by hard punches. Both her breasts were screaming at her to protect them from more punishment, but she focussed on offense and ignored the burning pain every time another fist slammed into her breasts.

Mindi's breasts were also constantly burning with pain, but she refused to show her opponent how much she was hurting them. She used her right knee to soften up the brunette's body, slamming it into her already bruised ribs every time her lover left them unprotected. While doing this, she patiently waited for another opportunity to throw an elbow. It came when the brunette over-balance while trying to land a vicious right hook. The blonde stepped in and slammed her right elbow into Alexa's unprotected jaw. Her lights went out, and she fell heavily into the mud, face first. The referee jumped in and stopped the blonde from attacking her downed opponent. He pushed her back to her corner before returning to where the brunette was trying to get back to her feet. When he reached the count of eight, the fighter was still unstable and her eyes did not fully focus.

'Nine …'

'You fucking dare not. Let us fight.' Alexa was furious.

'Are you sure?'

'Yes!'

'Fight!'

Mindi rushed in. letting her fists go. She caught her lover in the face, before Alexa grabbed hold of her and held on with all she had, while burying her head into her opponent's chest to hide it from her fists. The blonde lifted her right knee and bumped it into the brunette's ribs, but she could not break her hold. When the referee eventually broke them apart, Mindi landed a left to her opponent's right breasts. This brought her hands down and a straight right slammed into her mouth, drawing blood from both her lips. The brunette went down again. This time she sat in the mud, waiting a few seconds to clear the cobwebs before slowly getting back to her feet. As she did, the bell rang for the end of the first round. Mindi floated back to her corner, while Alexa slowly made her way back to hers.

'You have her. Just keep slamming your elbow into her face. Your knees to her ribs are also very potent, and keep smashing her tits.' Lisa was as excited as the rowdy crowd.

'My breasts are killing me. The bitch really went to town on them.'

'This will help.' Lisa pressed an ice bag against Mindi's bruised mounts.

Tessa told her fighter to stay out of range for a while until she regained her senses. But she could see Alexa had other ideas.

When the second round started, Mindi rushed in and got caught with a straight right to her left eye. This stunned her, and she had to step back. The brunette followed her and landed a well-timed combination to her nose and jaw. The blonde stumbled backwards into the crowd. Somebody unceremoniously pushed her back into the fighting pit, where she was met with a shoulder to her chin. Lisa could not believe how fast the tide had turned. Mindi was now the one on her back in the mud, trying to get her head clear. Although she had been stunned, Mindi was stable when she got back to her feet. She covered up when her lover rushed in with a flurry of punches. These mostly connected with her arms, but the last two slammed into her bruised breasts. The immense pain made her mad, and she unleashed her own flurry of punches, elbows and knees. The second knee to Alexa's ribs made the brunette winch with pain. She lowered her arms and left her face open to an elbow to her temple, knocking her onto her knees. The blonde lined up a knee to her defenceless lover's head, but stopped herself just in time.

Alexa was upset with herself. She had the blonde in trouble, but allowed her to turn the tables. She got up and waited for the eight-count to finish. This time, both fighters were a bit more cautious. They circled each other, shooting out jabs to test the distance between them. Mindi was the first to attack again. She stepped in and threw a left uppercut to her lover's right breast. It made the large orb jump upwards, causing lots of pain to the brunette. The blonde followed this punch up with a right-left combination, which were both blocked by her opponent. While her lover's defence was high, she threw another knee to her ribs. But Alexa threw a hard elbow at the same time, catching the blonde above her left eye. Both felt the impact of the other's attack, but Mindi was the one staggering backwards. She had to take three steps to catch her balance. Just as she got her balance back, she caught a flying knee to the chest, knocking her flat on her back. The bell rang for the end of the round before she got back to her feet. The bell did not quite save her, as she was always going to get up before the referee would count her out. But she was glad to get a break to recover.

'Okay, we now know she has some power as well. But you are hurting her more than she is hurting you. The knees to her ribs are paying off. She won't be able to take many more of those.' Lisa was wondering whether she should stop the fight. The two lovers were inflicting real damage to each other. She wanted neither of them to be seriously injured. But the bell rang for the next round before she could decide.

The two weary fighters slowly closed the gap between them. Both threw a few jabs, but neither wanted to commit too much. They stayed just outside the strike zone for the first half of the round. Both had success with a few stiff jabs, but neither truly hurt the other. Mindi lost her patience first. In her mind, the brunette was still ready to quit if she could land a few well-placed strikes. When she stepped in, she planted her left foot and swung her knee towards her opponent's ribs. But a straight right smashed into her mouth and nose, knocking her off balance. The knee connected, but with no power. The blonde stayed on her feet while blood dripped from her nose and lips. She swayed out of the way of another right to her face before throwing another knee. This one smashed into the brunette's stomach, winding her. Mindi jumped at the opportunity to knock her lover down again. She threw a combination of four punches, all finding their target, before she slammed another knee into the brunette's ribs. The pain was too much and Alexa took a knee to avoid more strikes to her ribs.

The referee had seen enough. He stepped in and declared an end to the fight via a technical knockout. Alexa was in too much pain to complain. Two ribs were cracked, and she needed medical attention. But in years to come, she would often tell whoever cared to listen that the referee stopped the fight way too early. All who watched the fight knew this was not true, but they also knew she would never admit she could not continue.

The crowd cheered while the six fighters all took a bow in the fighting pit. They were all amazed by the violence these women inflicted on each other, and the mutual respect and friendship they now shared after the fights. While Mindi and the medics took Alexa to the nearest hospital, Lisa and Tessa went back to the pub to mingle with the crowd and to recruit new fighters. This last part was much easier than they thought it would be. Female truckers and wives and girlfriends of truckers were lining up to find out how to join the club. Although most men in the audience had only seen the nudity and skilful fighting, many of the women had seen much more. They had seen a way to be free of society's strict ideas of what women were supposed to do. They had seen a way to experience an adrenaline rush unlike any they had experienced before and they had seen a way to release their daily frustrations in a brutal, but sane way.

Chapter 8 – Planning the Second Event

Lisa and Tessa signed nine more women after the fights and received many promises from male truck drivers to tell their wives or girlfriends about the club. Many spectators wanted to know when the next event would be. A few actually paid for the next event in advance to ensure they would get tickets. When it was eventually time for bed, Lisa was on a high and could not fall asleep. She got her laptop out and decided to make the next day a rest day. Although they now had fifteen fighters, only two of the nine new recruits had any boxing or MMA training. The others would have to get training before they could take part in events. This left them with eight fighters ready to fight in a month's time, but she doubted whether Alexa would be ready to fight so soon. It meant they were back to three fights only. She was sure they would have a sell-out crowd, and she really wanted to make sure there would be five fights for them to enjoy. Then it hit her. Some women would have more natural ability than others. Maybe she could spar with the seven new recruits without training to identify those who were naturally good at fighting. These could then be fast-tracked to fight in the next event as novice fighters. The crowd would still have three skilled fights, but will also see two fights with women still learning the craft. She captured all her ideas on her laptop to discuss with the other three founding members of the club before she captured the fighting records of the six women who had fought earlier that night. While doing this, she started rating their performances in her head. To keep track, she entered her rating next to the fight record of each fighter. For her, the best fighter was Mary, so she gave her a ten. Alexa and Mindi had a better fight than her own, so she gave each of them a nine. Although Mindi had beaten her lover, she thought their overall performance was so close to each other that she could not give Alexa a lower rating. She felt the same about her and Tessa's performance and gave herself and her best friend an eight each, while she gave Ellen a seven.

As previously planned, the four founders of the fight club held a short meeting over breakfast the next morning. Alexa had refused to stay in hospital, and although still in pain, had insisted on being at the meeting. While discussing whether they had to change anything for the next event, Lisa told the other three about her plan to have sparring sessions with the new recruits. All agreed that this and the two novice fights was a good idea to get more fights, but that the novice fights would only happen until they had enough trained fighters to have five skilled fights every event.

'I also updated all our fighting stats last night. While I did that, I gave each fighter a performance rating. Maybe each of you should do the same. I gave the woman I thought had the best performance a ten, and then nines, eights, etcetera for the rest. I gave more than one woman the same rating, but I think only one should get a ten. We can use the average ratings to make sure we pit women of equal skills against each other in the future. This will make for more exciting fights. I also believe it will be best for the safety of the fighters, as we will better avoid mismatches.'

All three women liked this idea, and each wrote their ratings on a napkin. Lisa then entered all these scores and shared the averages with the others.

'So, the highest rated fighter was Mary with an average rating of 9.75. Then it is Mindi with 9.25; myself with 8.75; Alexa with 8.50; Tessa with 8.25; and Ellen with 7.75. These are, of course, subjective scores, but I think it will help us better plan future fights.'

All four women were excited with what the future held for their fight club. Alexa and Mindi would find a venue for the next event and would decide on the best date between twenty-five and thirty-five days from the first event. Lisa and Tessa would continue recruiting and sparing with the new recruits to establish who of them would be ready to fight without the requirement of three months' training first.

After the other three had left, Lisa found two of her new recruits in the pub. They were twin sisters who had started driving just a few months earlier. They worked for another female driver who had a fleet of six trucks. The owner was in her fifties and had boxed in the original topless boxing club, but she was no longer interested in fighting herself. However, she brought her two female drivers to the first topless fighting event of the new club, to introduce them to a sport she had enjoyed so much as a young woman. The twins had loved the fights and had signed up immediately after the event. Lisa was very excited to have two more fighters in her weight class. She and Tessa had promised each other never to fight each other again, and she wondered whether they would get other opponents as small as them, or whether they would have to fight in a heavier weight class.

'When are you guys leaving?'

'We are taking a rest day today,' Erin, the older twin by seven minutes, answered.

'So am I. I told you last night that you need at least three months of boxing or MMA training before you may have your first fight for us. But we have decided to have two novice fights at the next event. I will spar with each of our new recruits to identify the four women with the most skills. They will then fight in the next event.'

'We are both good fighters,' said Erika. Erin and I have been in many fistfights, some against each other, but mostly with other women. The last was two weeks ago when the two of us had a fight against three strippers. All three were bigger than us, but we still kicked their butts.'

'Maybe I can spar with you today to gauge your skills?'

'You are in no state to spar. Give your bruises and cuts time to heal first. But the two of us can fight and you can watch.'

'Mmmm. Yes, maybe that will work. But we don't have any medics here, so no strikes to the face. You will spar for a few minutes only. If I am satisfied, you will fight at the next event. If not, you will have to get some training first.'

'Oh, you will be impressed with what you see.'

After chatting for a few more minutes, the three women headed back to Lisa's room. She handed the twins a set of MMA gloves each.

'Here?' Erin had a frown on her face.

'Yes.'

'It's too small. Let's go to the truck parking area again. We can fight in the same fighting pit you've used last night.'

'Most of the trucks are gone. It will be much easier for outsiders to see.'

'There is a clearing in the woods behind the parking area. I went for a walk yesterday. It is secluded.'

'Is it safe?' Lisa did not like the idea of going to a secluded spot in the woods.

'We both carry.' Erika lifted her shirt just enough to reveal her Walther PPS.

'Fine then.'

Lisa followed the twins into the woods. They followed a game trail until reaching a small stream. Erin turned right and followed the stream for a few minutes until they reached the opening she had mentioned earlier. It was not much bigger than Lisa's room, but it did not have any furniture in it. Lisa loved the setting. It was perfect for a fight. She wished they could use it for an event, but it unfortunately did not have any space for spectators. The twins handed her their pistols before taking off their tops and bras to reveal A-cup breasts with stiff brown nipples. The two brunettes helped each other to tie their shoulder-length hair into ponytails before they squared off. Before Lisa could remind them of the rules, they unleashed on each other's bodies with fists and knees. The two tiny sisters were fast and relentless, targeting each other's small breasts with their fists, while their knees smashed into each other's sides. Both kept to the rules, but the damage they did to each other's bodies concerned Lisa. She had no medics on standby and after Mindi had cracked two of Alexa's ribs, she did not want to take any chances.

'Ladies, break. I have seen enough. You are more than ready to fight at our next event.'

The twins broke on her command, but both were still in the mood for a fight.

'May we go for one more round?' Erin lifted her fists while saying this.

'No. I do not want either of you to get injured.'

'Let's wrestle then. I saw a small mud pit on our way here.' Erika was also eager to continue with some sort of contest against her twin.

'Okay, then. But you wrestle from your knees and I will break it up if you get too rough with each other.' Lisa could not say no to this. She was keen to see these two sexy sisters wrestle each other in a muddy pit.

The twins rushed back to where they had earlier seen their potential mud wrestling pit. Both stripped off their jeans, boots and socks to face each other in their panties only. Erin was wearing a baby-blue thong, while her sister wore a lacey yellow panty covering only the top part of her tight bum. Once they were down to their underwear, the two topless women rushed to the small mud pit, where they soon faced each other on their knees. Both giggled nervously before grabbing hold of her opponent. The fight was fast and furious. Both got the other down, but neither could stay on top. MTheir sexy petite bodies were soon covered in mud, making it even more difficult for Lisa to tell them apart. She thought about her grandmother and hoped she had enjoyed wrestling in the mud as much as these two sisters were. Although she had never slept with another woman, the sight of these two tiny sisters wrestling in the mud made her very horny. She was tempted to get naked in jump into the mud with them. But the sisters were having a very competitive wrestling match and she did not want to interrupt that. They wrestled for almost ten minutes before Erika managed to pin her sister for a three count. After the fight, both were sucking in huge gulps of air while sitting next to each other completely covered in mud.

'You got lucky. Next time your ass is mine.'

'All skills, sister. All skills, no luck.'

The sisters hugged each other after getting up. Lisa waited for them to clean up in the stream. She handed them their clothes and when they were dressed, their pistols. The two tired sisters were walking back much slower than she wanted to go. She wanted to get back to her room to release her sexual energy. When she eventually got back to her room, she stripped naked and recalled the images of the sexy twins wrestling in the mud, while her hands explored her own sexy body.

Chapter 9 – The Ambush

Early the next morning, Lisa started her truck, getting ready for a tricky route through a mountain pass. With a flask of coffee and a few sandwiches next to her for breakfast, she slowly pulled out of the parking area. As she joined the interstate highway, another truck pulled out of the parking area and followed her at a distance. This did not raise any suspicion with Lisa. Trucks often followed each other, especially when they were facing a dangerous route like the one she faced that day. She gave the truck behind her a courtesy call on the radio, but it did not answer. Once again, this did not raise any suspicions, as truckers were not always in the mood for a chat. Some men also still did not talk to female truckers, as they did not see them as fellow truckers. A few minutes later, she tried a channel she and her female trucker friends used when they wanted private conversations. It was, of course, not guaranteed that nobody else would be on this channel, but at least it was not one of the generally used channels. She was glad when Alexa's voice came back over the radio.

'Good morning, sunshine.'

'How are your ribs doing?'

'My ribs are fine. I told you the bitch hits like a girl.'

Lisa could hear Mindi laughing in the background.

'I found two fighters who are ready for our next event. The twins who signed up after our fights. They are little spitfires.'

'Great, the spectators would love to see twins fighting each other.'

'That was my first idea as well. But Tessa and I will not fight each other again. I am not sure whether we will get two more atomweight women who would be ready to fight us in a month's time. This means we are back to three fights only if the two of us do not have opponents.'

'Do you suggest they should fight the two of you?'

'Yes. They have good skills. I think they may be good enough to beat us. It will definitely not be a mismatch.'

'But the idea was to have novice fights.'

'I know. But we found two fighters who are ready. I think we should let them fight us. Maybe we can be in each other's corners for the two fights. You know, two friends fighting two twins. The second fight would almost be a grudge fight for whichever team has lost the first.'

'What about a two-on-two fight?'

'A free for all?'

'Maybe not. Still a one-on-one, but at the same time. We will have to think about how to make it work, but I think the crowd would love something different.'

'It sounds interesting. I will think about how to do it.'

'Maybe we should meet again soon.'

'Idiot!'

'What?'

'Not you. This bastard overtook me on a blind rise and had to squeeze in when another car came towards us. He made me slam on my brakes. Now I have lost all my momentum and am struggling to make it up the hill.'

'Is your camera on?'

'No. You know I dislike it.'

'It protects you when something like this happens. If you had gone into the back of him, it would look like you were the guilty party, unless you have video footage to show what actually happened. Switch it on.'

'Okay. You are right.' Lissa switched the front-facing camera on, while trying to ensure she did not stall the truck up the last few yards of the steep hill.

The truck following her had caught up with her and overtook her as soon as they crossed the crest of the hill. As they passed her, Amanda and Thomas glared over at her. Out of habit, she raised a hand to acknowledge them, but neither of them responded.

'Oh good. More assholes on the road,' said Lisa to herself. She allowed the other truck to open a gap on her, not wanting to be too close to the religious extremists.

The next hour was uneventful, and Lisa settled into the monotony of a quiet road. The other truck was out of sight, and she had not seen another vehicle for a long time. But she knew she would have to use all her skills soon, when she would start climbing the mountain pass. While the going was easy, she poured another cup of coffee and had one of her sandwiches. About a mile before the first climb of the mountain pass, she pulled over to ensure her truck did not have any issues which would force her to stop while climbing the pass. Once satisfied, she picked up speed to give her momentum for the first steep climb. All went well, and she reached the highest point without incident. However, going down the other side would be just as difficult and even more dangerous. She once again pulled off and inspected her truck, while having another coffee. The petite driver rested for a few minutes before slowly winding her way down the narrow mountain pass. After rounding about the fourth turn on her way down, she saw the religious fanatics' truck blocking her lane just before the next turn, with its hazard lights on. Although she did not like these people at all, she pulled up behind them and also switched her hazard lights on. The trucker code dictated that a trucker should always help another trucker who was in trouble. When she got no answer on the radio, she got out and walked towards their cab. The cab was empty, so she returned to her truck. As she turned back, she saw Amanda and Thomas waiting for her between their trucks. This scared her, but she acted cool.

'Do you have trouble with your truck? How can I help?'

'We don't accept help from a sinner.' Amanda moved to block Lisa's way back to her cab.

'I will be on my way then.'

'You are going nowhere, whore. We warned you to stop your depraved show. But you are determined to continue degrading women. It is bad enough that you insist on doing a man's job, but we will not allow you to have naked women fighting for the enjoyment of lustful sinners. God instructed us to punish you for the sins you are so determined to commit.'

'Get out of my way.' Lisa tried to push past the blonde, but the women outweighed her by over thirty pounds and easily blocked her, before giving her a hard shove.

The redhead almost fell, but stayed on her feet by taking several steps backwards. The larger woman followed her and grabbed a hand full of hair, while her other fist pumped into her opponent's face. Blood soon dripped from the redhead's nose, but this just made her mad. With her head pulled down by her hair, she could not generate much power, but a swift knee to the blonde's vagina did the trick. The larger woman released her grip on her opponent's hair, while shouting out in pain and shock. She was not ready for what followed. Lisa quickly followed her and landed a brutal elbow to the bridge of her nose, breaking it. When the larger woman covered her face, the redhead kneed her in the groin again. Sobbing uncontrollably, Amanda sank to her knees. Lisa was tempted to knee her in the face, but decided to use the opportunity to get back in her truck. But then her legs gave way. At first, she did not know what happened, but then she saw Thomas with a baseball bat standing behind her. The pain in her lower back then hit her. She was sure Thomas was about to hit her again and she tried to get away from him. But her body did not want to listen to her brain. Fortunately, he did not smash her head in like she feared. Instead, he used the bat to choke her, just enough for her to struggle to breathe. She grabbed hold of the bat with both hands and tried to pry it away from her throat. But the enormous man was too strong for her.

'Come, finish her. She broke your nose, break hers.'

Lisa could see in Amanda's eyes that she had no fight left in her. She had been defeated and did not want to fight anymore. But she also did not want to disobey her husband. She slowly got up with blood still dripping from her nose. Lisa could do very little to protect herself. When she covered her face with her arms, Thomas increased the pressure on her throat, forcing her to grab hold of the bat again. This left her face unprotected to a hard kick. After Amanda landed the first kick, Thomas yelled at her to continue. She landed a few more kicks to the petite woman's body before opening a cut above her left eye and breaking her nose with two hard kicks to the face. She stepped back, but her husband shouted at her to continue. After three more kicks to the defenceless woman's face, the larger woman turned around and walked away.

'That is enough. I am done,' she screamed, while tears streamed down her cheeks.

'Finish this! Come back and finish this!' Thomas was furious at his wife for disobeying him. When he realised his wife was not coming back, he moved the baseball bat away from the tiny woman's throat and allowed her to drop forward onto the ground. Before he returned to his truck, he landed two hard kicks to her ribs.

About ten minutes after the religious fanatics had left her at the side of the road, a car stopped. A couple rushed over to the beaten-up woman.

'What happened? Are you okay?'

'Please help me to my truck.'

'You cannot drive. We will call an ambulance.'

'Call the ambulance, but I need to get to my cab.'

The husband gently helped the redhead to her feet while his wife called an ambulance. Lisa winced in pain. She knew she had broken ribs and a broken nose. Moving on her own was almost impossible, and it was very difficult and painful, even with the help of the guy.

'What do you need in your cab? Let me rather get it for you.'

'Okay. Select channel four on the pre-set channels. Ask for Mindi, Alexa or Tessa. Tell them I have been beaten up by the religious nuts and that I am in bad shape. Tell them I need somebody to drive my truck to its destination. They know where that is.'

The guy helped her to the back seat of their car before he returned to the cab.

'Tessa, Mindi or Alexa, please come in.'

'Who is this?' Alexa sounded suspicious.

'My name is Frank. I stopped to help a woman. I did not ask her name. She asked me to tell you the religious nuts have beaten her up. She is in bad shape. We have called an ambulance and is waiting for it to get here.'

'How bad is she? Is it a petite redhead?'

'Yes. I think her ribs are broken. She is also bleeding from her nose and has other cuts to her face. My wife is trying to stop the bleeding.'

'You will see a control panel for the camera next to the radio. Please press the green button. You will have a choice to save the last five minutes, thirty minutes, hour or two hours. Please select the 'last two hours' option and save it.'

'Okay, I have done that.'

'Will you please download it to your phone and forward it to me?' Alexa gave him her number and waited until she received the file. 'Thank you. Please stay with her until the ambulance arrives. I will find drivers in the area to drive her truck to her offload destination.

Thirty minutes later, an emergency helicopter landed. The flight doctor and paramedic stabilised Lisa before loading her into the helicopter for transport to the nearest hospital.

Chapter 10 - Revenge

With her three friends all on the road, Lisa spent the first three days alone in the hospital. She was in pain and felt humiliated, running what happened to her through her head repeatedly, wondering what she could have done differently. 'Maybe I should not have taken on the religious extremists at the female truckers' fighting event. Just ignoring them was probably to better choice. But why should extremist be allowed to force their beliefs on others? No, I did the right thing to stand up for my friends. Maybe I should not have stopped. But what if they really were in trouble? What will happen if truckers stopped helping each other? Is our club a good idea? Maybe women fist fighting each other topless is slightly too sexy and violent.'

The more she thought about this, the angrier she became. These people had messed up her head. Things that had made so much sense to her were now in a grey area. She was no longer convinced the fighting club was a good idea. It was unsanctioned, and she knew no state commission would ever sanction it. Getting arrested was therefore a risk. It was a risk she had been willing to take. But now she was not so sure anymore. It would only take one person to spill the beans for her and her friends to lose everything, including their freedom. She felt controlled. Others were deciding for her whether she could fight, how she could fight and what she could wear. No matter what, she would not allow them to be the boss of her. She would do whatever it took to stop these religious extremists from taking away her freedoms. Justice would be hers. Revenge would be sweet.

On the third day in the hospital, two police officers visited her. Lisa immediately thought they were there to arrest her for running a female fight club.

'Your doctor reported an assault case. He tells us you have three broken ribs, a broken nose and many bruises, some older than the others. Did your husband do this to you?' The older male officer showed little sympathy. For him, this was just another case to solve. However, his young female partner gave her a sweet, sympathetic smile.

'I am not married.' Lisa was still concerned by their presence and her answer was short and semi-hostile.

'Who did this to you, then?' The older officer was quickly losing patience with her.

Lisa knew she could get the religious extremists into a lot of trouble. But this was not the revenge she was craving. She wanted to put both of them in a hospital. She wanted to break every bone in their bodies. This was not an issue for the police to resolve. This was personal.

'I don't know.'

'Give us something. Why did he beat you up? What did he look at?'

'It was road rage. We were probably both at fault.'

'You are wasting …' The older cop was irritated.

'Mike, don't you want to go talk to the doctor again?' The female cop interrupted her partner with a gentle tone. She waited until he had left before continuing. 'My name is Julia. If it will make you more comfortable, we can talk off the record. I am here to help you. This was not just road rage. You have older bruises as well.'

'I was in a fight the night before the road rage incident.'

'You do not strike me as the kind of woman who regularly has arguments with other people. What caused the other fight?'

'It was not like that. I had a friendly fight with a friend. We both wanted to have a fight, and we both enjoyed it.'

The female cop gave the trucker a knowing smile. 'You would not be involved with the trucker fight club, would you?'

'What do you mean?' Lisa's defences went up again'

'Don't worry. This is not a police enquiry. I ask this in my personal capacity. My boyfriend's family owns a few truck stops.

. He has told me about the topless boxing club of years gone by. The other day he told me that there are rumours somebody has revived the club. Completely off the record. Is this true?'

Lisa thought for a long time before answering. 'I may know what you are talking about.'

'So it's true. There has been a topless boxing club?'

'Yes, my grandparents started it with friends of theirs.'

'And did you ..?'

'Yes.' Lisa knew it was a risk to confirm that they started a fighting club. But she could not help but to trust the young policewoman.

'When I joined the police academy, a few of us had our own private wrestling club. But boxing sounds very exciting.'

'It used to be a boxing club. Our club also allows knee and elbow strikes.'

'Be careful. Serious injuries may put you on law enforcement's radar.'

'We all train, and we have medics at our events. If you want to …'

'What?'

'I will have to talk to the rest of our committee first. The club is only for truckers.'

'Did you want to invite me?'

'Yes, but the others may not like it if I bring a cop with.'

'My boyfriend is a medic. He may also be able to arrange events at some of his family's truck stops, if you need another venue.'

'I will talk to the others. But if you come, it will have to be as a civilian.'

'I am excited. But back to business. Are you sure you don't want to tell me what really happened on the mountain pass?'

'I am sure.'

'Please don't retaliate. I would hate to arrest you.'

Lisa just gave the female cop a smile. Sometimes you meet somebody and you become instant friends. Julia was one of these people. She could not help but to like the young cop, and she was sure the feeling was mutual.

Lisa could hardly contain herself when Tessa walked into her room. In her excitement, she moved too fast and immediately regretted it. The pain from her broken ribs was intense.

'I don't care what your story is, I will tell everybody you ended up in the hospital after our fight.'

'I'm sure you will, bitch.'

'Not a good idea to call your almighty conqueror a bitch.'

'If I was known for my good judgement, I would probably not be in here.'

'Have the police caught those bastards yet?'

'No. I did not tell the police who did this to me.'

'Why not!'

'I will deal with them in my own way.'

'Are you mad?'

'After what they've done to me, they deserve all I plan to do to them.'

'You are in no shape to do anything. And even if you manage to hurt them, you may end up in jail. Let the police deal with them.'

'No. They need to understand what I felt like while they were beating me up. I want them to go through the same fear and pain.'

'I cannot allow you to do this.'

'Let's talk about something else. I do not want to fight with you.'

Tessa was not ready to drop the topic. But she knew her friend. It was a waste of time to continue the argument. She would have to give her time to think about this before trying to convince her again.

'So, am I your first visitor?'

'Yes. Well, the police were here. The female cop seems to be very interested in our fights. I am thinking of inviting her to one of our events.'

'Now you've gone completely mad. A cop will shut us down. We will all end up in jail.'

'Not this cop. Her boyfriend is a medic and his family owns a few truck stops. She will not come as a cop, but as a fan of the sport.'

'I don't know. It sounds way too risky to me.'

'If you meet her, you will agree with me. She is a nice woman, and she definitely loves female fighting.'

'You may be right. But it is still a risk.'

Two days later, the lesbian lovers visited Lisa in the hospital. This time, she did not try to raise her upper body when they entered.

'It's okay, don't get up, lazybones', said Alexa with mock sarcasm.

'Why would I, after getting used to nurses serving my every need?'

'This sounds like my kind of hospital. I have many needs', said Alexa with a naughty smile on her face.

'Careful what you wish for. If you look at any of the nurses, I may just crack a few more of your ribs.' Mindi winked at her lover.

'So, Tessa tells me you want to go after the couple who did this to you?'

'Yes.'

'I get that. But we have to be clever. They might do anything to close us down. We don't need anybody to report our club to the police. With the video of the assault, we hold all the cards. We can use that to make sure they focus their extremist hate at somebody else.'

'I can't believe you want to negotiate with these people. I want to stop them from ever trying to force their believes on anybody else.'

'That is noble. But you cannot stop extremists not to hate. We have the tools to stop them from bothering us, though.'

'I will have to think about it.'

'Good. Tessa also tells me you want to bring a female cop to one of our events. I understand she likes female fighting.'

'Yes, but you do not understand…'

'I think it's a good idea. To be honest, I think we should invite her to fight.'

'Why?'

'If she has a fight, she could never report us. Also, getting a cop on our side may help should somebody ever report us.'

'You want to use her?'

'I want to rub her back with the understanding that she might have to rub our backs in the future.'

'That does not feel right.'

'We will give her the choice. She will know exactly what we expect from her.'

'I will talk to her. But I like her, so I don't want to put her in an awkward position.'

'Set up a meeting with her. I will give her all the facts. She can then make her own decisions.'

Chapter 11 – Agreements

A few days after her friend had visited her, Lisa left the hospital, with strict instructions not to drive her truck for another three weeks. The doctor also told her not to take part in any physical activities for at least three months. Knowing that she could not fight during at least the next three events depressed her. But it also motivated her to ensure the next event would be an enormous success. When Alexa had suggested that they should convince Julia to fight, she had not liked the idea. But after thinking about it for a few days, she actually loved the idea. However, there were a few issues they had to figure out first. The first was the rule that only female truckers and truckers' wives or girlfriends could fight for the club. The second was how to manage the reaction from other truckers should they learn that a cop knew about the underground fight club. A few ideas formed in Lisa's mind for the first issue. They could change the rules to allow them to invite guest fighters. Another alternative was to get Julia to drive her truck while she could not do so. During one of their phone conversations, the young cop had mentioned that she had driven a breakdown truck for her family's one truck stop for a short period after finishing school. Lisa was not sure whether the young woman had a license to drive an eighteen-wheeler, so she called her. After greeting each other, Lisa got straight to the point.

'I talked to the other founders about you attending one of our events. As you may imagine, they have concerns because you are a cop.'

'I understand that. But I promise I will come in my personal capacity. You know I will do nothing which may cause your club to be shut down.'

'I know. One of them suggested you should fight. This way, they can be sure you would not bring any charges against us and the club.'

'Me fight? Are you sure?' The policewoman sounded very excited.

'Yes. Is it something you would consider?'

'Off course. I would love to fight.'

'Do you have any experience? We only allow women to fight if they have at least three months' training, or if they have enough natural fighting skills.'

'We received boxing and grappling training in the academy. I still spar regularly to keep my skills sharp. We never know when we will have to fight. Many people resist when we take them into custody.'

'Good. We have another issue, though. The club rules only allow female truckers and wives and girlfriends of truckers to fight.'

'Are you asking me to be your girlfriend?' The young cop laughed at her own joke.

Lisa also laughed before answering. 'No, but if you have a license, maybe you can drive my truck while I cannot. It will only be for quick trips and only on your off days.'

'I have a license. Let me talk to my sergeant. We need permission to moonlight.'

'Great. I will pay you off course.'

'Thanks. I wish I could tell you not to worry, but extra cash is always handy on a cop's salary.'

'I would not have it any other way. Talk to you soon then.'

'I will let you know tomorrow.'

The next afternoon, Julia phoned and confirmed she could drive Lisa's truck. After noting down the cop's schedule for the next few weeks, she started phoning for short haul opportunities. After securing four transport opportunities over the two weeks, she phoned Alexa and told her about the recent development.

'That is great. Who will she fight?'

'She is about my size. Maybe she can take my place in a two-on-two against the twins.'

'That sounds good. I have news as well. I got hold of Thomas and Amanda. After I sent them the footage of them assaulting you, they have agreed to sit down with us. They are in your area later this week. I will make sure we are also there. Let me know which day and where and I will make the rest of the arrangements.'

Lisa was quiet for a few seconds. She did not know whether she was ready to face the religious extremists. 'I will let you know.'

'Don't worry. We will be there. They will not touch you again.'

'Thank you.'

Three days later, Lisa and Julia headed towards a town a few hours away for a delivery. Afterwards, they met Alexa, Mindi and Tessa at the local truck stop to discuss the meeting later with the religious extremists. Lisa introduced the young cop to her friends before they discussed the upcoming meeting.

'We will all be with you. As chairperson of the club, I will do the talking.

We will keep it short and to the point. Do not get into any arguments about the merits of our club or whether women should drive trucks or fight. We do not care about their views. What we want is an agreement that they will leave us alone, and that we will not lay charges for assaulting you.' As usual, Alexa had applied her mind and was ready for the meeting.

'May I sit in as well? I will not tell them know I am a cop, but I will defuse the situation should it get out of hand.'

'You are welcome if Lisa wants you to sit in.'

'Yes, I do.'

'Settled then. Shall we go?'

The women took a taxi to the pub where they had agreed to meet. When they arrived, Amanda and Thomas were already seated at a table in the corner, away from the other patrons. Thomas logged eyes with Lisa, shooting her daggers of contempt, while his wife cast her eyes downwards, looking embarrassed and uncomfortable. When the woman sat down, Lisa ensured she sat right across from the couple, looking directly at them. Thomas was still looking at her with hate in his eyes, but Amanda could not look at her.

'Thank you for meeting with us. Our aim is to reach an agreement with you. We do not want any trouble in the future. This means we will not lay any charges against you for assaulting Lisa, and you will no longer try to shut down our fighting club. Do we have an agreement?' Alexa immediately took control of the meeting.

'How do we know you would not lay charges, anyway?'

'We all have much to lose. We just want to do what we love. I am sure you also just want to carry on with your life without the fear of going to jail.'

Thomas wanted to argue more. Although he knew the women were generous with their offer, he wanted to have his say. 'You are sinners. It is my duty to show you the errors of your ways.'

'Our offer is simple. You leave us alone, and we will leave you alone.'

'I cannot …'

'You do not seem to understand. We are not here to discuss your views. We are here to make a deal with you. Decide if you want this deal.'

'I need to go to the bathroom.' Amanda looked Lisa straight in the eyes while saying this. There was sadness in her eyes.

Lisa waited a few moments before she also got up to go to the ladies' room.

'Where are you going?' Thomas sounded concerned.

'I also need to go to the bathroom.'

'Stay away from my wife.'

'Nothing will happen. I will go with her.' Julia also got up.

Thomas wanted to argue further, but the women did not give him a chance. They turned and walked to the bathroom. Amanda was waiting inside. She looked very nervous and tears rolled down her cheeks.

'I am so sorry for what we have done to you. It was definitely not a Christian thing to do. After that day, I have thought a lot. I have been a Christian for a long time, and I will always be a Christian. But the way Thomas interprets the Bible no longer makes sense to me.'

'Does he hit you?' Julia asked this with a tender voice.

Amanda could not answer. Instead, she started sobbing. Lisa immediately hugged her, holding her tightly until she calmed down enough to talk again.

'He made me believe I deserved the beatings and that it was his duty to discipline me for sinning. I no longer want that, but I have nothing and cannot get away from him.'

'I can help you, but only if you are ready to be helped.' Julia's voice was still sympathetic, but stern enough for Amanda to understand she had to do her part in order to be helped.

'I want to get away, but I have no work experience.'

'We have programmes to help you learn new skills. Do you have children?'

'No.'

'That makes it easier. With children we would have to get the courts involved, but without, he doesn't have any hold over you, and he will not know where you are. I ask you again, are you ready to do this?'

'I have to. Yes, but he will be very mad if I try to leave him.'

'Do not worry about his reaction. I am a police officer. If you are sure you are ready to go, I will call for backup. By the time he realises what is going on, there will be nothing he could do about it.'

The other two women waited in the bathroom while Julia phoned the local police station. Afterwards, the three women returned to the table. Thomas was clearly irritated.

'Why did you take so long?'

'I am leaving you.' There was a lot of fear in Amanda's voice. She remained standing and moved away from him when he got up.

'What! How dare you!' Thomas got up and tried to grab hold of his wife.
Julia was between them in a flash. The battered woman was not supposed to
say anything. She had to wait until backup arrived before leaving with
them. But her premature action had now put the tiny policewoman in a
tough spot. She had to handle the massive man without backup. But she was
not on her own. The four friends all stood beside her within mere moments.
Alexa, Mindi and Tessa did not know about the plan, but they saw Thomas
was about to attack the small policewoman and they all reacted
instinctively.

Although two of the women were recovering from busted ribs and other
injuries, Thomas was not keen on fighting these women. He had seen them
fighting and he knew that, unlike his wife, they could defend themselves.
'We had a deal.'

'We still do. This is something different. You will never hit Amanda again.
She had enough and is leaving you.' Lisa looked straight into the huge
man's eyes while saying this.

'I am a policewoman. Your wife is coming with me. Sit down, or I will
arrest you.' Julia took her badge from her pocket and showed it to the man.

For a few moments there was a tense stand-off while Thomas contemplated
his options. He was not prepared to let his wife go. In his mind, she
belonged to him and had to do whatever he told her to. But he was not one
to hit a woman if she was willing to hit back. And the five women facing
him down were all very willing to hit back. 'Can't you see what these
sinners are doing? The devil is using them to drive a wedge between us. He

is targeting your weak female mind. Stop this nonsense now, while I am still willing to forgive you for your weakness.'

'This is not weakness, asshole. She is standing up to you after years of abuse. This is pure strength. You are too weak to carry on without her though. I can see it in your eyes.' Lisa took a step towards the man, but Tessa pulled her back.

'Stay out of this bitch. You need a good man to put you in your place.'

'Do you want to try?'

'This is my last warning. Sit down, or I will arrest you.' Julia stepped between Lisa and Anthony. 'Take her outside until backup arrives.'

Anthony looked at the young cop for a few seconds before following her instructions. Only when he was seated did Lisa accompany Amanda outside. They waited until two police vehicles arrived before going back inside. Two uniformed policemen sat down with Thomas to keep him from interfering, while two more talked to Amanda and Julia at another table. After getting all the facts, they took them back to the precinct, until social services arrived to take Amanda into a shelter for abused women in an undisclosed city.

Chapter 12 – The Second Event

Helping the woman who assaulted her had been the last thing on Lisa's mind when they had their meeting. But now that she helped Amanda get away from her abusive husband, she felt empowered and motivated to help more abused women. Over the next few weeks, she talked to Julia about programmes available to these women and potential opportunities for her to assist some of them in starting a new life. She was also very impressed with the young cop's driving skills and work ethic. On top of this, the young woman had a very positive outlook on life and a wicket sense of humour, which was tough on Lisa's ribs. Although it hurt every time she laughed, she could not wait for the next funny comment. With the next event around the corner, she used the days when Julia had shifts as a policewoman, to make the required arrangements for the event.

A few days before the event, Lisa and Julia were in the same area as Tessa. They arranged to meet up for lunch at the local truck stop. Lisa was very excited to see her best friend. She also hoped that Tessa and Julia would hit it off, as she enjoyed spending time with both of them. But there was an unexpected coldness between her two friends. She realised she had spent little time with Tessa, and when she did, she had talked a lot about how great Julia was. While in the cabin of her truck with Julia, she had talked a lot about how great Tessa was. Subconsciously, she had probably hoped to convince them to like each other. But it now became clear to her that she achieved the opposite. Both women were slightly fed-up with the other, and slightly jealous of the other.

Lisa tried to ease tensions by joking around, but neither of her friends was in the mood for light-hearted banter. Instead, they were sparring with verbal jabs at each other. It all came to a boil when Tessa made a derogatory remark about weekend truckers.

'Are you calling me a weekend trucker?'

'If the shoe fits.'

'Well, a real trucker would settle this with me outside.'

Tessa immediately got up, and so did Julia. Lisa tried to stop them, but realised she was just making both more upset with each other. She followed them outside, and so did the rest of the patrons, excited to watch a female fistfight. The two women were ready to fight the moment they got outside. But Lisa convinced them to move to a lawn, rather than to fight on the cement path between the lodges and the entrance to the truck stop pub. Both women removed their shirts while walking to the lawn. Lisa took the shirts from them and made sure she was between them when they reached the lawn.

'Do either of you want any rules?'

'No, we fight until one of us verbally gives.' Tessa lifted her fists while saying this.

'Agreed.' Julia also lifted her fists.

As soon as Lisa stepped away, the two tiny women started throwing. Fists smacked into each other while the small crowd cheered them on. Both landed to the other's face, but it was Tessa who got rocked first with a left to her chin. Her legs wobbled, and she stumbled forward into her opponent. By pure instinct, she wrapped her arms around the young cop's body. Having hurt her opponent, Julia wanted to continue punching, but their close proximity made it difficult to land any power strikes. The blonde recovered quickly and sank both her hands into her opponent's short red hair, pulling down hard while moving her feet slightly backwards before slamming a knee into the young cop's face. She tried a second knee strike, but Julia grabbed hold of her thighs and bundled her over. With blood dripping from her nose, the redhead held on to her opponent's legs, while burying her head into her tummy to regain her senses after the hard knee she took to her face. The blonde scooted backwards, trying to get free. But when she realised her opponent was holding on too tightly, she grabbed hold of her hair again with her left hand, while slamming her right fist into her head. Although she could not generate much power, the strikes still hurt and after taking a few, Julia reacted. She released her hold on the blonde's legs and scramble forward to get on top of her. While doing this, she grabbed hold of the truckdriver's bra and broke the right shoulder strap while pulling down on it. This exposed the blonde's beautiful B-cup breast and erect brown nipple. But guys getting a good look at her perky breast, was the last thing on the blonde's mind. She pushed a hand into her opponent's face to stop her from mounting her. But the redhead was strong and determined, and soon her chest pressed down on her opponent's chest. While scrambling for position, Julia's B-cup breasts popped out of her bra. Her stiff pink nipple jousted with her opponent's erect brown nipple for a moment, while their naked breasts pancaked each other. Both women felt a tingle of excitement. Their eyes met for a fraction of a second, to confirm whether the other also felt it. But both immediately returned to their fight for position. The redhead pressed an elbow into her opponent's throat, while trying to get up onto her knees. But as she brought her knees forward, the blonde bucked her body while twisting it to her left. The young cop lost her balance and fell forward. This gave Tessa an opportunity to get back to her feet.

Both women took a moment to remove their bras, which were no longer covering their breasts, but just served as a hinderance. A murmur of excitement spread through the small crowd watching the two topless women squaring off to resume their fight. Both were breathing heavily, and both were determined to knock the living hell out of the other. Fists slammed into flesh as both unleashed fury on the other. There was little to choose between the two tiny fighters. Both landed, and both were taking a lot of punishment. Something had to give, but neither was willing to take a step backwards. When they got very close to each other after a violent exchange, both grabbed hold of the other's hair with one hand, while pummelling each other's faces and bodies with the other. As they tired, the frequency of punches and the power with which they were thrown reduced significantly. Lisa waited until there was a long break between punches before she stepped in. She placed a hand on each woman's shoulder.

'It is enough now. You have both taken out your anger on the other. Let's go get the two of you cleaned up so I can patch up your cuts and bruises.'

Both women let go of the other's hair and stepped back. They were too tired to argue with their friend.

'Okay guys. The show is over. Get back to your drinks. If you want to see more of this, buy tickets for our fight club events.'

Lisa handed her two friends their shirts before walking with them to reception to book a room where they could clean up and talk this out in private. Once in the room, she realised she needed to fetch her first aid kit from her truck.

'I want the two of you to shake hands. The fight is over and I do not want any further hostilities between you.'

The two women shook hands and then gave each other a slightly awkward hug.

'Good, stay here. I need to go fetch my first aid kit. If either of you starts any trouble before I am back, I will fuck you both up.'

Lisa rushed to her truck, grabbed the first aid kit, and rushed back. To her surprise, she found her two friends naked in the shower, kissing each other passionately.

'What the fuck?'

The two women either did not hear her, or they flatly ignored her. She stood around awkwardly for a few moments before dropping the first aid kit on the bed and making her way back to the pub for a drink. About two hours later, her two friends joined her, looking slightly sheepish.

'Really! After all that hostility, you end up sleeping together?'

'You know. There was a spark, even during our fistfight. When we stripped down to shower, our breasts touched and one thing led to the other.' Tessa shrugged her shoulders, as if this was just a normal love story.

'So, you beat the shit out of each other and then make love?'

'Not exactly. We decided we still had to settle our differences, so we had a sexfight with each other.' Julia also said this as if this was what women usually did after having a catfight.

'A sexfight?'

'Yes, you know, we saw who could make the other one come first.'

'May I ask who won?' Lisa could not hide how aroused she was by this.

'She won two rounds. I won three.' Tessa looked proud of being the sexfight queen.

'Five times?'

'The loser kept challenging the winner. We only stopped because we felt guilty for leaving you here on your own.'

'Thanks, I guess. I assume you are then still happy to fight the twins?'

'Bring them on. We will fuck them up.'

'As long as you don't have sexfights with them afterwards.'

'Maybe we will.'

All three women laughed before Lisa gave each of them a long, tight hug. 'I am so glad you two are friends now. It broke my heart when you fought each other.'

'Oh, we plan to fight again. But this time in the fighting pit at one of your events.'

A few days later, the women arrived at the truck stop early. While the others were booking in, Alexa met with the owner to ensure everything was in place for their female fighting event that night. The man was excited to have the event at his truck stop, knowing that it would bring in lots of business. He took her to the area he had prepared for the fights, in the centre of the overnight parking area. They had already parked the trucks around the fighting pit, the way Alexa had explained to him. Between the trucks, he had laid down grass blocks to give the women a more forgiving fighting area.

'We will have a mini fridge with ice-cold drinks, chairs for the corners and fresh towels.'

'Thank you so much. This looks fantastic. Will there be guards at the gates tonight?'

'Yes. They will also scan the police frequencies to ensure an unexpected visit will not surprise us.'

'That is great. I am sure it will be an epic event tonight.'

'I hope so. I also hope you will use our facilities often in the future.'

'If all goes well, we will.'

Julia was nervous. Her boyfriend would arrive soon to do duty as a medic at the female fighting event. When she and Tessa had their sexfights, she thought it was just a once-off sexual experiment. But over the past few days, she had developed feelings for the truck driver. She wanted to pursue a relationship with her, which meant she had to break up with her boyfriend. But she did not want to spoil his fun and decided to break up with him after the fights. Although she wanted to be with Tessa, she spent the day trying to avoid her. But this was impossible. First, Alexa and Lisa arranged a meeting for all the fighters to discuss the fights and any special rules any of the opponents agreed to. During this meeting, Tessa sat down next to her.

'I think we should ask for a rule change. Our fight will currently be a team contest, with two one-on-one fights at the same time. Maybe we should do this for the first three rounds, but then have a two-on-two fight for the last two rounds.'

Julia liked this idea. 'Maybe we should combine the last two rounds, and fight them without a break.'

When they suggested this rule change, the twins immediately accepted it. They also wanted a brawl where they could team up against one opponent when such an opportunity presented itself.

After the meeting, Alexa introduced the fighters to the truckers, having a drink in the pub. Julia saw her boyfriend for the first time that day during this meet-and-greet. He was visibly excited about seeing her and the other women fighting topless. Seeing him like this made her decision to break up with him even more difficult. He was a good guy, and she did not want to break his heart. But she knew she would only string him along if she did not break up with him as soon as possible. She almost broke up with him there and then, but once again decided to only do it after the fights.

Soon, it was time for the first fight. As Alexa and Lisa could not fight, they acted as corner women, and Alexa also did all the announcements. She waited until the crowd, of just over a hundred men and women, all found a spot from where to view the fights before she announced the first fight.

'Ladies and gentlemen, welcome to the Truckers Female Fight Club's second event. Tonight, we have five fights for your entertainment. The first fight is our first team contest. Two teams of two women each will face each other in a striking match. They may to strike with fists, elbows and knees. The first three rounds will be three minutes each and we will have two one-on-one fights happening at the same time. Round four will be a five-minute round, and we will have a two-on-two fight. This means a team may gang up on one fighter when her teammate is knocked down. The fighters may also change opponents at any time. If a fighter is knocked out, she may not re-join the fight when she regains consciousness. A team will win when they have knocked out both their opponents. If this does not happen, the team with one knockout will win. If there are no knockouts, or one knockout each, the team with the most knock-downs will win. There will be no additional time. Therefore, it will be a draw if the teams are equal on knock-downs after the fourth round.'

The trucker smiled because the crowd cheered each rule she shared with them. It was clear they were excited to witness some hard-fought female fights.

'Please welcome our first team, two friends, Julia and Tessa.'

The crowd went wild when the two tiny women made their way to the fighting pit. Julia noticed the concern on her boyfriend's face. This woke the butterflies in her tummy. Like many men, he had been dreaming about the day he would watch his girlfriend fight another sexy woman. But now, he was scared she could get injured. The rules of the fight allowed for a much more violent fight than the ones he had been imagining in the past.

'Please welcome the second team, the twins, Erin and Erika.'

The cheers were even louder than for the first team. Many in the crowd loved the idea of twins fighting. Although they would prefer to see them fight each other, they were still looking forward to see them fight as a team. Alexa nodded to the referee as soon as all four women were in the fighting pit. He called them to the centre and quickly reminded them not to kick or wrestle and to obey his instruction. When they returned to their corners, all four petite women removed their leather jackets before putting on their MMA gloves. The cheers increased in volume again, this time for the twins, who had stunning little bodies and pretty faces. The two brunettes had tied their shoulder-length hair in two ponytails, making them look playful. Their brown eyes were full of confidence and determination, though. Both had bright red lipstick on their full lips and a subtle amount of blush on their high cheekbones. Their A-cup breast worked perfectly with their small bodies and were adorned by thick brown nipples, standing proud in anticipation of the upcoming combat. Their flat tummies were well defined and the sparkly bellybutton rings drew the eyes to their sexy midriffs. The tight jeans they were wearing for the fight showed off their shapely thighs and calves, and their tight bums.

The two women across the fighting pit from them were no less sexy. Julia's Pixie style red hair and green eyes, combined with her small nose and thin lips, gave her a striking look, even with minimum makeup on. Tessa's long blonde hair was tied in one ponytail. Like her teammate, her makeup was subtle, used only to highlight her blue eyes, high cheekbones, and sultry lips. Both of them had perky B-cup breasts with prominent nipples. Sixpacks were clearly visible on their flat tummies. Like their opponents, they were wearing tight jeans, which showed off their athletic legs and tight bums.

The referee waited for the applause to settle down slightly before he called all four fighters to the centre of the fighting pit.

'Ladies, this is a one-on-one fight for the first three rounds. This means you may not interfere with your teammate's fight in any way. If your opponent goes down, you may not strike her. Obey my commands at all times. Do you understand?' He waited until all four women nodded before continuing. 'Go back to your corners and come out fighting when I tell you to.' Once he was satisfied all four ladies were ready to fight, he gave them the instruction to start.

For the first round, Erin and Tessa squared off, while Erika and Julia did the same. Lisa wanted her two friends to win the fight, but she also liked the twins, so she decided to only give advice between rounds and not to shout advice during the rounds. Alexa, who was in the twins' corner, had no such qualms, though. She encouraged the twins to beat up her long-time friend and the young cop, whom she liked a lot.

The twins came out fast. Each crowded her opponent and swung their fists with power. Tessa moved well and avoided most of these punches, while landing a few of her own. However, Julia got caught with a hard punch to her jaw and was on the back foot early in the round. Erika did not give her any respite, and soon had her backed up against the crowd, who acted as the ropes for the fighting pit. With nowhere to go, she planted her feet and swung back with all she had. But her head had not completely cleared yet and her opponent soon landed another solid punch to her chin. The redhead went down, falling into the crowd. The woman behind her tried to catch her, but only managed to twist her around, making her fall face first into the grass. Tessa could hear the count, but there was no time to look over at her downed teammate. She and Erin were both landing with fists, knees and elbows. Although their strikes hurt, neither could get the other in trouble.

Julia got up at the count of six. She still felt slightly dizzy and her legs felt heavy, making it difficult for her to move the way she wanted. When the brunette came forward, she grabbed hold of her to give herself more time to recover. With the referee having to watch two fights, she stayed in the clinch for longer than he would normally allow. But this also allowed her frustrated opponent to land a short knee to her vagina. The sudden pain forced the redhead to let go of her opponent, just as the referee turned his head in their direction. Another knee to her midriff and an elbow to her forehead sent her crashing down again. This time, she barely made it back to her feet before the count of ten. The referee gave her an extra few seconds to recover by ensuring she was fine to continue. This time, Erin kept her distance, throwing a few jabs to keep the redhead away from her. Every time she wanted to move in to throw a hard strike, it looked like Julia was going to grab hold of her again, causing her to hesitate.

On the other side of the fighting pit, Erika and Tessa were still pummelling each other. Both were bleeding from the nose and both had visible bruises on their bodies. They were a good match for each other, resulting in a very exciting fight. Both stayed in the pocket, throwing with all they had. When the referee called the end of the round, their bodies were covered in sweat.

Lisa waited for her friends to sit down before giving them advice. 'Julia, use this time to recover fully. You got caught early. It happens. Take your time. Fight from behind your jab until you find your timing and distance. Tessa, you are doing well, but be careful, you are taking too much punishment. Move more. Try to avoid her strikes by keeping your distance. Only move in when you see an opening. She will come in. Counterstrike and move away.'

For the second round, the twins switched opponents. At first, their opponents did not realise this. But, although it was very difficult to tell them apart, the first round had left much more bruises on Erika's body. Julia realised she had a different opponent first. Erika seemed more determined to hunt her down than her twin sister had been. This gave the redhead, who recovered from her earlier knockdowns, many opportunities to land strikes. She used mainly stiff jabs, but also landed a few knees and elbows. But the harder she landed on the brunette, the more the twin hunted her down. Tessa found Erica was more cautious than her sister. This gave her time to fight her fight, moving a lot more than she had done during the first round. All four women landed solid strikes during the round, but none of them could put their opponent down.

Between rounds, Lisa told her fighters that they had done well and to build on their successes during that round. Feeling that they had had less success in the second round than in the first, the twins switched back to their original opponents. For Erin and Tessa, the round was much the same as the first round. Although Tessa tried to move more, she got drawn into a brawl again. The crowd loved this exciting fight, cheering on both fighters. But the fight between Erika and Julia differed greatly from what it had been during the first round. Julia was moving well, making sure she did not get caught by a wild punch again. She was landing regular strikes, and although she was also on the receiving end of some strikes, she was getting the better of the twin. At about ninety seconds into the round, she landed a left knee to the brunette's solar plexus and followed it with a hard elbow to her temple. The knee winded her, while the elbow disrupted her balance, forcing the tiny woman to stumble to her right before falling on her side. She tried to get up immediately, but was still disorientated and fell down again. This time, she took a few seconds to recover before getting back to her feet. Julia immediately closed in on her and threw hard punches at her head. The twin managed to avoid most of these, but went down again when a solid right smashed into her chin. She stayed on her knee until the last second before getting up. After the referee ensured the brunette was fine to continue, the redhead quickly closed the gap between them again. But this time Erika grabbed hold of her and refused to let go, even when the referee ordered her two. He had to pull them apart. But after eating two punches to the face, the twin grabbed hold of her opponent again. This frustrated the young cop. She decided to repay her opponent for the illegal knee strike she had received during the first round. The short knee to the crotch did the trick, forcing the brunette to go down. But the low blow did not go unnoticed. The referee immediately stepped in.

'This is your last warning. No more low blows.'

'But she did it to me first. You said nothing then.'

'This is not a debate. Do not do that again.'

He allowed Erika time to recover while the fight between Tessa and Erin continued. Both of them had taken lots of punishment and they were having trouble staying on their feet. But both were also exhausted and could not land a power strike. The round ended just after Erika indicated she was ready to continue fighting.

Lisa went into the fighting pit to help Tessa back to the corner. 'Remember, it will now be a two-on-two fight. Julia, you are much fresher than Tessa. I need you to go after Erin and to knock her out. She could hardly stay on her feet at the end of the last round. Tessa, stay out of trouble. Clinch if you have to. Erika will have much more energy than you have. Do not stand with her. As soon as Julia puts Erin down, the two of you must go all out to knock Erika out as well.'

Alexa had a similar plan for the twins. Erika attacked Tessa with all she had, while Erin tried to stay away from Julia. But the young policewoman hunted her down easily and unloaded with all she had. When the twin tried to grab hold of her, she caught her with a vicious elbow to the face. The brunette went down, falling flat on her tummy. While the referee started his count, the redhead headed towards where Erika and Tessa were fighting. The blonde had ignored Lisa's advice and was trading strikes with the twin. When the redhead joined the fight, the twin had no chance. She could not avoid strikes from two opponents and soon went down from an uppercut to her chin. But her sister had beaten the count and was walking towards her two opponents with her fists raised. Like her sister, she stood no chance against two women. She fought valiantly, throwing with all she had. But a few hard punches to her small breasts brought her defences down. A barrage of punches and elbows to her head, put her down again. This time, she stayed down. As Erika also did not beat the count, the fight was over. The victorious friends gave each other a tight hug before locking their lips in a passionate kiss. The entire crowd, except for Julia's boyfriend, cheered them on. When the young cop remembered he was watching them, she broke the kiss and headed over to him.

'I am so sorry. The kiss was not planned. I wanted to tell you after the fights to ensure you would enjoy them.'

'What is this? Are you a lesbian now?'

'I don't know. But I know I am in love with her. I need to pursue this. I am so sorry you had to find out like this.'

The young man looked at her for a few seconds before shaking his head. 'How can you do this to me?'

'I never meant to hurt you. This just happened. I was not looking for it. But my feelings for her are too strong to ignore.'

'Were you lying about your feelings for me?'

'No, I will always love you. But I have to follow my heart. I know this will be awkward for you, but I want you to watch the other four fights.'

'How can I enjoy the fights now?'

'I am going to my room. There will be sexy topless women fighting. Focus on them. We can talk again when we both had time to deal with this.' She turned around and headed for her room, trying to keep the tears at bay, but failing miserably.

Her boyfriend stood around for a while, contemplating whether he should watch the rest of the fights. But he could not deal with his emotions and decided to rather leave.

With only one medic left at the event, Lisa and Alexa considered cancelling the rest of the fights, but decided against it. This would later prove to be an excellent decision. The following four fights were classics. The crowd could not believe how much skills and guts these women had. Years after this event, truckers still talked about it, although there were many excellent events in the years to come. Lisa watched the fights with a smile on her face. She knew she had started something very important for women who enjoyed fighting. She could not wait to get back in the fighting pit, to test her skills against other like-minded women.

The End